Merry's Christmas

a love story

SUSAN ROHRER

Infinite Arts Media

MERRY'S CHRISTMAS: a love story
Written by Susan Rohrer
Adapted from Rohrer's original screenplay

Kindly direct all professional inquiries about screenplay or novel to:
InfiniteArtsMgmt@gmail.com

Readers may contact author at:
shelfari.com/susanrohrer

Cover Image: Courtesy of Indigo Valley Photography
Author photo: Jean-Louis Darville (with permission)

ISBN: 1479147095

Published in the United States of America

First Edition 2012

To every heart

that hangs onto hope

in the miracle that is Christmas

contents

one
❧ ♥ ❧

Perhaps it didn't make sense to throw open the window and let the scant heat of a drafty studio apartment escape into the brisk December air. But for Merry Hopper, responding to the fullness of her heart trumped what made sense to most other people on a regular basis.

No matter what anyone thought, said, or did, and most especially on this particular morning, everything in Merry sang out in celebration. This was the season—her season. She knew it, with a conviction just as dependable as the elevated train rumbling by hourly, as certain as the rent she had no way to pay, and as insistent as the calico cat at her feet, meowing for breakfast.

"There they are, Rudy!" she exuded, scooping up the feline for a peek out the window. "Look. See? It's already starting."

Indeed, just across the street, city workers bustled about, festooning the eaves of the train station with machine-wrought pine boughs and enormous extruded bows. Clearly, the decorations had weathered many a year, but the sight of their return was still a welcome reminder of the coming Yuletide season.

Even though Merry had been both born and abandoned on Christmas day almost twenty-nine years prior; even though she'd been bounced around the foster care system without ever having a family to call her own, Christmas was a time when Merry liked to think that all the world was celebrating her birthday, too. Jubilantly, she threw open the sash.

"Merry Christmas, Mr. Grabinski!" Merry called out, the winter blast whipping through her well-worn pajamas.

Fastidious to a fault, the apartment super barely looked up, compulsively sweeping balsam and pine bits into neat little piles on the walk. "Merry Schmerry," he groused. "I'm barely picked up from

Thanksgiving and already they got needles all over creation."

Suddenly, Merry's eyes widened incredulously. It couldn't be happening, but it was. Just beyond Mr. Grabinski, a stocky, middle-aged man leaned over the business end of a tow truck. He was well into hooking up a faded red Volkswagen Beetle.

To call the vintage Bug red was, at most, a generous way of acknowledging what the color once was, long before the oxidation and saltings of too many Chicago winters had had their way with the paint. Still, it was Merry's—almost paid for with her meager base as a waitress. It would be all hers in just a couple of months, if holiday tipping measured up to her hopes.

"No!" Merry cried. "No, no, hey that's... Wait!"

Merry ducked inside, disappearing from the window, finally motivating Mr. Grabinski to peer up to her second story walk-up, where tattered curtains billowed out of the abandoned portal.

"The window, Merry!" he bellowed. "I'm not heating the whole free world!"

Hearing him, Merry circled back to close the window, and then dashed through her humble dwelling. She scrambled to throw on a coat that had seen far too many seasons, knocking an overflowing box of decorations onto the floor in the process.

"Wait, wait, wait... I'm coming!" Merry shouted, as she leapt over her calico cat, Rudy, and ran out of her apartment, down the stairs, and out the front door.

At curbside, the tow truck guy continued to secure Merry's Beetle to his rig, undeterred by her protests, which resumed in earnest the moment she burst from the building.

"Mister, please, I'm good for it! I get paid this afternoon!"

"Then, you can take it to the impound," he grunted.

"Come on, it's Christmas time," Merry tried, "How am I supposed to get around?"

The expression on his face told Merry that this guy had heard it all. What was worse, he refused to look at her. "Sounds like the upside of living under a train," he cracked, locking off the car.

Merry was well accustomed to dealing with grouchy men. She had a way of breaking through the even gruffest of hearts to the soft, gooey center underneath. "Please," she implored. "Okay, okay, just... Come on, look at me like a human being in completely genuine need and don't do this."

Finally, he turned to her. For a moment, it seemed he might relent. "No, you look at me," he barked. "I don't take the Bug, I don't get paid, then I got nothin' at all to put under the tree for my kids this year."

Merry stopped in her tracks. She had a soft spot for kids, especially kids who had to do without, the way she'd had to do for so many years. "But..." Merry continued, her conviction to fight for herself waning as the man headed toward the cab of his truck. She followed him as he plopped into the driver's seat and stuck his keys in the ignition. "Seriously? Kids, huh?"

"Five."

Suddenly, everything in Merry flip-flopped. She did look at the tow truck guy. She looked at him hard. He didn't seem nearly as heartless as he had at first. He wasn't her enemy. He was just a dad, working a thankless job in a tough economy to put food on the table for his family.

"Just take it," she sighed.

And take Merry's car, he did. Without another word, he started the truck and puttered away with Merry's not-so-very-red Beetle bouncing along in tow behind him.

Merry watched, defeated, as the only thing of value she almost owned disappeared into the distance. It was like losing a friend of sorts, and she promised herself that somehow she'd get it back.

Merry turned, mortified that Mr. Grabinski had observed the entire incident. "Monday's the first," he reminded. "You got rent."

Merry pulled her coat closed. "I know, I know," she assured.

Merry scurried back to her apartment and closed the door, choking back tears. Her cat, Rudy, studied her. He was that special kind of animal that seemed to understand when her life got to be overwhelming.

Outside the vintage Downtown Diner, Skeeter Jeffries held up a cardboard sign that read: "Will Work for Food. God Bless You!" Merry kept an eye out for Skeeter through the plate glass window while she worked. He was a daily reminder that there were those who faced challenges even greater than hers.

Pedestrians routinely passed Skeeter by, refusing so much as to make eye contact. But over time, Merry had watched Skeeter as he'd developed something of an arms' length relationship with the diner's regulars, and how they'd come to be good for bits of loose change after they'd filled their own growling stomachs.

Merry had gotten to know Skeeter over the four long years since he'd been laid off from his job with the city's Sanitation Department. A younger man might have found another position, she realized. But Skeeter was near retirement age and had long since accepted his lot in life. He had acclimated to making his way on the street and to the cardboard box behind the diner that he had come to call home.

Inside the diner, Merry waited as the barrel-bodied owner and short-order cook, Arthur Biddle, stacked freshly grilled hotcakes onto a plate. Merry had known for a long time that Arthur wasn't one to do the niceties. There might have been an unrefined gruffness to his exterior, but in Merry's experience, Arthur had always been a stand-up guy. He'd given her a job when she needed it and a helpful hand on more occasions than she could count.

"My offer, it still stands," Arthur announced, scooping a dollop of butter onto the steaming stack of cakes.

As nonchalant as he was about it, one would have thought Arthur was referring to an advance on Merry's pay or an arrangement for vacation time. But Merry knew exactly what offer Arthur meant immediately. It wasn't something they talked about. They hadn't spoken a word of it since the day Arthur had first flipped those Four Words onto the table.

He hadn't gotten down on one knee. There had been no candlelight dinner or romantic stroll on the waterfront. Merry knew that, with Arthur, there was no pretense. He was a no-frills guy. You saw exactly what you got. He had said those Four Words a woman longs to hear in the kitchen of the diner, his forearms shiny with grease, in the process of yanking the giblets out of a turkey's hind parts.

Taken off guard, Merry had brushed it off, as if Arthur must have been kidding. She'd tap danced her way around really answering back then, not wanting to hurt his feelings or to make things too awkward at this job she so desperately needed. But this time around, as casual as Merry tried to keep things, she knew she owed the man an actual answer.

"Arthur, you know I adore you—"

Arthur shook his head. "Yeah, I can hear that *but* rolling up. But. But this, but that. That's what you're gonna say, am I right?"

"I'm gonna say that, I just—I'm in this crazy-making situation and—I'm not going to marry to solve a problem, Arthur. I kind of want to marry for love."

"Who says love ain't a problem?" Arthur asked. The man was way smarter than he looked.

♥　♥　♥

Far across town in a decidedly upscale bistro, Daniel Bell leaned over the remains of Eggs Benedict to kiss his date, Catherine Strong, goodbye. As he pulled away, she lingered.

"You know what your problem is, Daniel? You're pathologically responsible, that's all."

Daniel straightened up congenially and signed to cover the check. As beautiful as Catherine was, he found her coy wit to be every bit as appealing as her pale blue eyes and her lithe, feminine form. Rising, he stroked Catherine's arm affectionately. "Much as I hate to tear myself away, I'm sure your father would appreciate it. 'Tis the season, you know."

As Daniel rose to leave, Catherine checked her lipstick. "Daddy shouldn't work you so hard," she pouted.

"I do believe he's testing me."

"Grooming you," Catherine corrected. "There's a difference. He's been hinting about retiring."

Daniel had supposed as much.

At seventy, Catherine's father had been dialing back time spent at the office gradually. The president of the bank that had stayed in his family for generations, Catherine was his sole heir and the apple of his eye. A shrewd man, he'd begun to entrust more and more responsibility to Daniel, with a not so subtle approving nod toward the developing relationship between his star vice president and his one-time jet-setting daughter.

It had seemed strange at first to Daniel. As a widower of almost three years, Daniel hadn't dated or even desired to for such a very long time. It had been all he could do to function after losing his wife. Suddenly a single parent, he had thrown himself into his work, which was precisely where he'd eventually met Catherine, fresh off a break-up and ready to keep her feet on the ground for a while. Finally, the cloud of grief had lifted for Daniel, and his lonesome heart had found a way to move on again.

"Would you be up for an early dinner?" Daniel inquired.

"I believe I could swing that. Could we try someplace new?"

Daniel smiled knowingly. He steeled himself to take the plunge. "Actually, I was thinking my place. It's time you met the children."

♥　♥　♥

Arthur dished up an order of hash and scooted it up on the counter for Merry. "I'm just saying."

Merry wiped something sticky off her hands. "And I appreciate it, Arthur, but—"

"Your point is that I ain't 'It'."

Merry put her towel down, leaning closer in earnest. The last thing she ever wanted to do was to hurt Arthur, but she didn't have an insincere bone in her body. "No, no, you're undeniably It. Your Itness is legend. I mean, you're fabulously It for somebody. And you're way It as a friend for me, but—"

Arthur gestured toward the waiting order. "Hash ain't getting any hotter."

Merry grabbed the plate and delivered it to a man at the counter as fellow waitress Kiki Stone sidled up to her. African-American and in her early forties, Kiki had a winning way of diving straight for the bottom line. "How much you short?"

Merry waved her friend off. "Keep it, Kiki. You're feeding your boys by yourself. I'll figure it out."

Undaunted, Kiki cheerily emptied the tips from her pockets. "Not gonna deprive me of my blessing. Nuh-uh. Mama always said, 'Give and it shall be given to you, pressed down, shaken together, running all over the place.' So, you best take what I got, get that whole Christmas ball rolling."

Leaving no room for Merry to protest, Kiki picked up a pitcher of ice water and sashayed back out to the floor. Merry glanced at the pile of cash. Kiki had a knack for racking up tips and this particular morning had been no exception.

"Go on, there's more where that come from," Kiki waved, already across the diner. Gratefully, Merry collected Kiki's earnings and stuffed them into her apron.

Later that day, Merry spun through the revolving door of Strong Bank & Trust. There was something about revolving doors that left her a little off balance, even after she'd escaped one's orbit. Regaining her equilibrium, she scanned the vaulted ceilings and the elegantly appointed lobby, suddenly self-conscious about her uniform. Not far from the entrance, she saw a man, apparently in his late thirties, shaking the hand of an impeccably dressed elderly socialite. A uniformed driver stood at the woman's side.

"I'm Daniel Bell," the man said. "It'll be my pleasure to handle your accounts, Mrs. Rockingham. Here's my card."

It's not that Merry noticed every man who crossed her path, but for some reason there was something about this Daniel Bell that caught her attention. Maybe it was just overhearing his name, she thought. Maybe it was the pleasantness of his voice. It might have been how professional he looked in his perfectly tailored suit. Whatever it was,

Merry reasoned, he seemed like someone who could help her.

As Merry waited, she glanced down at the coffee cup in her hand. She kicked herself for not throwing it away in the trashcan on the street corner. It's not that it was empty. It's just that a paper cup seemed incongruous in this place, so she checked around for a place to toss it.

As Mrs. Rockingham grandly passed to exit, Merry turned to clear the woman's path to the door. There were times it seemed that Merry's timing was impeccable. This wasn't one of them. As it was, when she backed farther into the lobby, she smacked right into Daniel. Startled, she whirled and, to make matters worse, coffee from the aforementioned coffee cup sloshed onto Daniel's charcoal suit.

"Oh!" Merry gasped. "Oh, no, I... Let me—" Flustered, Merry quickly used her napkin to blot Daniel's jacket.

"It's fine," he assured. "Really. I've got it."

As Daniel took over the wiping, Merry couldn't help but notice how congenial he was being about her gaffe, or how very handsome he looked in his freshly stained jacket.

"I'm so sorry," she said. "Could I get that cleaned?"

Daniel smiled, putting a hand up in polite refusal. "No, no. Needed it anyway. Is there something I can do for you?"

Chagrined, Merry piped up. "You wouldn't know where I could get a loan application, would you?"

Night had long since fallen and, with it, the Downtown Diner had closed its doors for the evening. Skeeter cozied up to a heating vent just outside the front plate glass window.

Inside, Arthur put chairs up on tables while Merry sat, studying the paperwork from the bank. With all its blank lines gaping at her, the form was more than a little intimidating. Merry had always done her best to pay her bills on time. A time or two she'd cut it close. Never before, though, had she had a repossession that she would have to declare.

Not until that morning.

The voice Merry didn't like to listen to sorely tempted her to leave the smudge off her application. It was a voice she'd heard more than once in her life, enough to recognize the grimy pit of its origins. It rationalized omitting the humiliating truth that, try as she might, she'd failed to make her November payment. It taunted her to worry what that nice man at the bank would think of her when he saw what a deadbeat she was.

Merry sat, motionless. She thought about the times she'd listened to that nagging voice. She pondered how empty she'd felt whenever she'd given into it. Finally, she shook her head *no*. She took a deep breath and put her pen to the paper.

"I could help you with that loan app," Arthur offered. "Best reference you'd find. That don't change, just 'cause you don't go for what I got."

Merry looked up with sheepish affection. "You're like a big brother, Arthur."

"Big as in too old? That it?"

Arthur always nailed it on the head. As much as Merry attempted to save his pride, he always saw through it. "Kinda hoping to stay in my decade," she admitted. "Still love you, though."

Arthur shrugged, and then flipped another chair over onto a table. "I'll co-sign that if you need it."

Merry felt awful. How could Arthur be so completely great to her even though she was rejecting him? "I couldn't—"

Arthur stopped. "So, you love me like a brother. Whaddaya think brothers do?"

♥ ♥ ♥

Daniel entered his high-toned kitchen, stopping a moment to take in the aroma of barbequed chicken. There was his mother, Joan—still fit at sixty—husking fresh corn on the cob. His fashion-forward fifteen year-old daughter, Tara, was in the process of making a salad, and her sardonic twin sister, Hayden, pecked insistently on a laptop. It was the new normal they'd found as a family since what they rarely talked about.

"You're home early," Joan slyly observed. "You must be terribly interested in this girl."

"She's a woman, Mother," Daniel replied.

Joan brushed the correction off. "I'm as liberated as the next one, but honestly, Dear. What woman doesn't appreciate the implication of youth?"

"I don't," Tara complained. "Not when I can't car date."

Joan gave her granddaughter a consoling squeeze. "Trust me. You'll be older soon enough. Enjoy your youth for the two seconds it lasts."

"And by all means," Hayden goaded, "rub it in as often as possible that you have a boyfriend who wants to take you on a car date."

Tara rolled her eyes, completely unamused.

Daniel scanned the faces of his girls. "I hope I can count on you to remember your manners tonight. You, too, Mother."

Hayden simultaneously slumped and groaned. "Tell me we don't have to like her."

Daniel tried his best to be patient. He knew that their mother would be a hard act to follow by anyone's standards, even his own. "You could be open," he suggested. "I know she'll never be your mom, but...I like her."

Suddenly, Tara showed interest. "You mean you like her, like her?"

Daniel wasn't one to blush, but he did take a second to compose himself. "Yes. For the record, I like her, like her. Run upstairs and change for dinner, will you?"

Already stylishly garbed, Tara flashed a playfully indignant glare. "Excuse me, Dad, but...please."

With a nod, Daniel acknowledged Tara's very suitable attire in contrast to her sister, Hayden's. Hayden shook her head and rose compliantly.

"Silly me. I thought I'd just wow her with my witty repartee."

"Which is always appreciated," Daniel added.

"Yeah, in Geekville—" Hayden began, just as her nine year-old brother, Ollie, burst into the room.

Jubilantly filthy, Ollie ran straight to his father. "Dad, can I start a worm farm?"

"—population: two," Hayden concluded as she disappeared up the kitchen stairs.

Daniel turned to his son. Ollie was always popping with ideas, a new one it seemed, every day. "I suppose that's negotiable," Daniel started. "But right now, how about you hit the shower? I have a date coming."

Clearly, Ollie was unimpressed. "More girls?" he moaned. "We're already surrounded."

"Just one," Daniel clarified, leading his son to the kitchen stairs.

Visibly engaged at the prospect, Joan probed. "Are you saying this thing is exclusive?"

Daniel turned back with a congenial sigh. "Try to contain yourself, Mother."

two

❧ ♥ ❧

Far across town—quite literally on the other side of the tracks in her single apartment—Merry strung lights around a tabletop Christmas tree. It didn't matter to her that she was the only one who would ever see this tribute to the season. She was used to spending the holidays solo, except for her cat.

Rudy watched, batting a paw at the dangling light string. Merry swayed side to side as she worked out a tangle, while Christmas music scratched on her radio. There was something about trimming a tree and listening to carols that buoyed Merry's spirit. It kept her hope astir that life wouldn't always be this way. She wouldn't always be working so hard, struggling just to barely make ends meet. She wouldn't always have to accept Kiki's hard-earned tips to keep Mr. Grabinski off her back about the rent. She wouldn't always be alone.

"What do you say, Rudy old boy? Look good to you? Maybe a little higher here." Merry picked Rudy up and stood back with him to admire her work. It wasn't anything fancy. The ornaments weren't store bought. They were pieced together with scraps of felt, loose buttons, shells, and colored glass beads, small treasures gathered by a girl who knew the true meaning of the Yuletide season, one who was quite sure that anything made with love was worth much more than all the store-bought Christmases in the world.

"Now, we're set. Come here, baby. Okay, moment of truth." Merry stepped over and, with a celebratory flourish, she flipped the light switch. Disappointingly, only about half of the bulbs lit. One sparked a few times before the whole string started to flicker, and then went completely dark.

"Perfect," Merry sighed.

♥　♥　♥

The clinking of lavish dinnerware did nothing but accentuate gaping pauses in the Bell dining room. No matter how much Catherine tried to tell herself that she wasn't responsible for carrying the conversational ball, she couldn't help feeling that she should. She smiled lightly at Tara. "That's a pretty ensemble you're wearing, Tara. You have an eye."

Tara readily responded. "I'm thinking of going into fashion."

Catherine caught Daniel's reassuring glance. "Really?" she replied. "I have a friend who's a buyer. Very chic, high end. Could mean contacts."

"I already wear lenses, but thanks," Tara replied cluelessly.

Daniel was quick to intervene. "I think Catherine might have meant the other kind of contacts. People in the fashion business."

Tara darkened sheepishly. "Oh."

Again, silence reigned.

Catherine counted the seconds that passed. It seemed an eternity. *Where were the witticisms that usually came so easily?* She searched her mind for something to say, anything to ease the awkwardness.

Finally, Daniel piped up. "Hayden is quite the computer aficionado, you know."

Hayden grimaced. "Yeah, I'm a real techno marvel."

"Designed and built her own website," Daniel continued. "Maybe she'll show you."

Hayden was expressionless. "Yeah, I can help you with your Facebook page."

As collected as Catherine was among adults, she felt herself faltering. "Yes, well... I'm afraid I don't actually—" She caught herself, finally getting Hayden's cynical drift. "You were being facetious, weren't you?"

"Attempting it," Hayden droned.

Ollie twirled spaghetti on his fork. "I'll show you my worm farm. If Dad lets me have one."

Grateful for the interaction, Catherine turned to the boy. "Oh, thank you. Is that what you want for Christmas?"

It seemed an innocent enough question to Catherine. In fact, she reassured herself it was. But Catherine quickly realized that somehow she'd managed to step in it once again. *But how?* All she knew was that, as soon as she'd mentioned the holiday, uncomfortable glances had darted amongst the family. She saw Joan shake a discreet head at her, warding her off the subject.

Catherine flushed with embarrassment. She'd never tried so hard to fit in or found herself failing so miserably. "I'm sorry. I seem to keep saying the wrong thing," she said.

"We don't ever have Christmas," Ollie blurted.

"Not anymore," Tara muttered.

Even Hayden chimed in. "Not since what we never talk about. More to the point, *who* we never talk about."

Joan tried to intervene. "Honey, maybe your father would rather—"

Daniel respectfully silenced his mother. "Actually," he began. "I... You know, I've been thinking about it for a while, now. Since last year, and it seems to me like it's about time we brought Christmas back again. That is, if that's okay with everybody."

Ollie lit up immediately at his father's suggestion. "With presents and everything?"

Catherine breathed a sigh of relief.

"All the trimmings. And don't worry, Mother," Daniel assured. "Lord knows, you do enough already. I'll take care of it. It'll be good. For all of us." Then taking her hand in his, he added, "Catherine, too."

Abruptly, Hayden got up from the table. "Imagine my joy."

Joan reached for Hayden as she skulked by toward the stairs. "Hayden—"

Daniel quietly turned to Catherine. "You okay if I...?"

Catherine promptly acquiesced. "Of course. Please."

Quickly, Daniel followed Hayden up the stairs.

No one said anything at the table. They just picked at their dinners, the silence more conspicuous than ever.

Catherine resolved not to take the floor again. She blotted her lips, then picked up her fork and began to eat, if for no other reasons than to fill the aching void. Within the privacy of her thoughts, Catherine did what she could to bolster her flagging confidence. She told herself that, in time, the children would get used to the idea of a new woman in their father's life. Surely, they'd come to know and love her, just as Daniel had.

♥   ♥   ♥

Across town, Merry paced about, on the phone in her apartment, a maxed-out credit card in hand. Holiday muzak lilted through the line. Rudy brushed against her leg, hinting that he wanted attention. She gathered him up into her arms and sat down on her bed. She scratched between his ears, just the way he liked it.

How long have I been on hold?

Merry checked her watch. Seven full minutes had passed since she'd been asked if she could wait just a moment and the never-ending loop of muzak had begun. *What is the definition of a moment?* She wondered if she'd been forgotten, if her call was nothing more than a blinking light on some abandoned who-knows-where switchboard that no one would ever notice again.

Merry was used to being cast aside. Her mind drifted back to her childhood, to the orphanages and foster homes of her youth, to the time or two when it had seemed that a couple might actually adopt her. How was it that so many years had passed and yet it seemed like yesterday?

The thought of how she'd once been chosen for a home visit floated into her head. She remembered it all, how she'd gotten up before the birds to scrub herself clean. She'd brushed her teeth for two whole minutes and combed every last snarl out of her unruly curls.

A social worker had driven her all the way out to the country, to a little white farmhouse with a dark red door and a sprawling apple orchard in the back. The people who lived there had seemed so nice. They'd had plenty of questions and she'd answered them as politely as she could. She'd played with their little boy and been shown the room that she would have gotten to share with their daughter. There had been a macaroni and cheese lunch with homegrown tomatoes and snap beans they'd just

picked fresh from their garden. When the time had
come to say goodbye, the lady had hugged her what
seemed like a very long while. She remembered how
they'd kept waving at each other, till the van pulled
out of sight.

For weeks afterward, Merry had kept her heart
on hold. She had waited and hoped for a reply that
never came. The social worker had explained things
as well as anyone could. It wasn't Merry's fault, she
said. People wanted babies, little children with no
memory of a time when they weren't part of a
family.

Merry switched the phone to her left ear and
sighed. Yes, she was well accustomed to being
abandoned, but the fact that it was the story of her
life didn't make it any easier in the financial crunch
of her here and now.

Abruptly, the muzak on Merry's phone line
clicked off. The disembodied voice returned,
mechanically quoting the company line.

"Yes, I understand your policy," Merry tried,
"but I'm in a little pinch now and...I know I'm at my
limit. I can't tell you how acutely aware of that I am,
but I was wondering, praying actually, that you could
up my limit. Just a few hundred dollars to get
me...No, I don't have anybody I can...Okay, thank
you."

Merry hung up. She spoke to the phone in sheer frustration. "Why am I thanking you?"

♥   ♥   ♥

Outside in the driveway, Daniel opened the door of Catherine's silver Mercedes, stealing a glance at the living room window from which his entire family monitored his not-so-private goodnight.

"We seem to have an audience," Catherine observed with a bemused grin.

"Apparently," Daniel agreed.

Catherine apologized again for her faux pas in mentioning Christmas. She explained that she'd hadn't realized that the topic was off limits.

Daniel felt for her. He knew the evening couldn't have been easy. He just hadn't realized it would be quite as hard as it had been. "No, it's fine," he reassured, not entirely believing it. "It's a fair assumption after three years."

Catherine nodded softly. A moment of silence passed between them. "Are you still...?"

Daniel took time to run the question over in his mind. He wanted to be completely honest with her, even though it was hard to explain. "We got through the worst of it the first year, but then Christmas rolled around again the next year and nobody seemed ready to..." Daniel trailed off, searching for words. "Then same thing last year. It's just, with losing their mom during the holidays, it's been a while since the kids have felt like celebrating."

Catherine took Daniel's hand. She intertwined her fingers with his. "The kids. What about you?"

Again, Daniel took a moment, wanting to be sincere. He thought about what he couldn't say, then gazed into Catherine's eyes warmly and offered what he could. "Suffice it to say, I'm in the mood to celebrate now."

♥ ♥ ♥

Merry knelt down beside her twin bed. Rudy curled up lazily beside her. Her elbows sunk into the thin batted mattress, making it pop up on the sides. Her hands clasped at her chin, Merry looked up, in earnest.

"So...is it okay to admit that I'm just a teensy bit freaked? Me and Rudy, here, we're cutting it kind of close. But I was wondering maybe, if—"

Merry's eyes filled. They teared the way they always did when she talked to the only Dad she'd ever known, the one who knew her best of all, the only one she could turn to and say whatever it was, no matter how terribly she was doing.

"Lots of people worse off than me, I know," Merry acknowledged respectfully. "I don't mean to ask for extras. Really, I don't. Just enough to get by. That's all I want this year."

The next morning, Merry made her way toward the train station. It was a new day, she encouraged herself, filled with new possibilities. She reminded herself that there really was an upside to living so close to the tracks, especially now that she needed public transportation.

"Spare some change?" a bag lady pleaded.

So in need herself, Merry passed the woman, then stopped and turned back. She dropped some of what little she had into the woman's cup and wished her a Merry Christmas.

"Merry Christmas to you, too. God Bless you, Miss!" the woman waved cheerily, flashing a rotten-toothed grin.

If that woman who had nothing could find reason to smile, Merry resolved that she would, too.

Entering Strong Bank & Trust wasn't quite as daunting for Merry the second time around. She had remembered to toss her coffee cup outside at the corner receptacle, and she navigated the heavy revolving door with quite a bit more ease. Spotting

Daniel's now familiar face where he sat behind a handsome mahogany desk, Merry took at seat in his waiting area. He was on a call, so she took the time to gather herself.

Things had been tight for Merry before, but never so dire that she'd had to ask for a loan. She pulled out her loan application and smoothed over the folds. There was her entire financial history, summed up in less than three pages. Showing this to a stranger was a little like walking down a hospital hallway, she thought, like wearing one of those thin cotton gowns that gapped disconcertingly in the back.

Merry watched Daniel. She listened as he talked on the phone. Absently, he wound up a tiny, toy robot, then released it to march across his blotter.

Daniel shifted the phone on his ear. "Yes...The sooner you can run it the better...Tomorrow morning's paper would be great...Yes, it's—"

Merry watched as Daniel picked up a note. She listened as he read from it.

"It should read: *Help Wanted: Christmas Coordinator. Full Service shopper, decorator, and event planner for family. $7,500 salary, all expenses advanced.'* That's it."

Merry's jaw dropped. She tried not to betray the fact that she had been eavesdropping, but nothing in her could help it. Maybe she was meant to overhear this, she reasoned. Maybe this was the answer to her prayers. She listened intently as Daniel continued on the call.

"Right. Then, just go with the blind e-mail box for replies...Absolutely...Sounds good."

Mouthing a quick *thank you*, Merry shoved her loan application into her bag and skidded up to Daniel's desk. In fact, she got there so quickly that she had to put her hands down to slow her momentum and stop her from crashing right into it.

"Could I possibly persuade you to cancel that ad you just placed?" Merry gasped.

Daniel looked up. "Do I know you?" he asked.

"I'm Merry Hopper. M-E-R-R-Y as in Merry Christmas, which is perfect because I really, really want that job." There. She'd said it with total conviction, knowing it was completely true.

Daniel smiled in a way that said he remembered her from their first encounter. "Merry. Oh, right. Aren't you the one who—"

"—spilled coffee all over you? Yes," she admitted. "That would be me. So, could I buy you a cup to actually drink this time?"

Life could change on a dime, Merry thought. One moment she could be completely down and out and the next, before she could even get her balance, she could be whip-lashed into what seemed to be an absolute miracle.

Merry reflected upon how quickly it had happened. Not ten minutes before she'd been ready to mortgage her future. Now, she was sitting at an upscale café, living in the possibilities. Merry watched as Daniel ordered his coffee from an uptown waiter. It was a far cry from the place where she worked.

"Espresso. Black," Daniel said. Then turning to Merry, he assured, "And this is my treat. Would you like anything?"

"Just to give your family the best Christmas ever," she beamed.

The fancy waiter nodded, bowing almost imperceptibly as he left, the way no one ever bowed at the Downtown Diner.

Daniel turned to Merry. "So, it's not huge...I have three children: twin girls, almost sixteen, a nine year-old son. There's my mother, who helps out with meals and such since my wife passed."

Immediately feeling for him, Merry interjected. "Oh, I'm sorry. So, your mother lives with you?"

"Practically. But no, she has very nice condo down the block."

Merry smiled. "Must be great to have her so close."

"Yes, well, she'd be very much included," Daniel went on, maintaining a professional tone. "May I ask, what kind of experience do you have for this kind of thing?"

Yikes, Merry thought. There it was, that gulpy moment. There was the temptation to embellish. But if this was the miracle it seemed to be, Merry knew she would come by it honestly. "I don't have any actual experience for this. So, none."

Daniel looked at her quizzically, prompting her to continue.

"But that's what makes me perfect for this job. I've been dreaming of throwing a family Christmas all my life. I just never had the family to do it for."

Daniel sat back cautiously. "I take it you're not bonded. I'd be setting up a dedicated account for my coordinator to draw upon for expenses."

"Arthur, he runs the diner where I work. He'll vouch for me," Merry assured. "I never stole so much as a single penny in all my life."

Shaking his head unconsciously, Daniel back-peddled. "Yes, well..."

"I won't lie, Mr. Bell," Merry promised. "I don't just want this job. Truth is, I really, really need it."

Daniel studied Merry for a moment, visibly torn by the decision.

As the waiter arrived with Daniel's promised coffee, Merry rose and stuck out her right hand. She knew that the practice of shaking another person's hand had fallen somewhat out of fashion, what with all the germs going around. Still, Merry responded to the urge to end things on a personal note. She knew she had little in terms of technical qualifications, but giving things a special touch was her forté. So, she shook the hand he extended warmly before turning to leave.

Merry stepped out into the brisk early December wind. She filled her lungs and left the café, quietly ecstatic. It wasn't an immediate *yes*—not by a long shot—but it also hadn't been an instant *no*, a fact that didn't escape her relentlessly hoping heart. This, she encouraged herself, was a definite *maybe*. There was a whisper of a chance, and Merry knew it. She had gotten her foot barely into this door and the windows of possibility had blown open.

three

Arthur hoisted a sack of bread flour onto his stock room shelf. Merry lingered nearby. In a way, Arthur enjoyed her attention. He knew Merry wasn't standing there because she'd heard anything about the Christmas Coordinator position yet. He'd seen her squeak back into the diner moments before her lunch break was over. There had been no jubilant announcement about this pipe dream of a job she'd spoken of actually coming true.

Arthur decided that, for once, he wouldn't make this easy for her, the way he usually did. Why should he? He was the one who'd been there for her all these years. He was the constant in her life. He would make her work for his attention for a change.

He'd keep futzing around, unloading cans, and straightening shelves. He'd pretend to only halfway listen. It was hard not to let himself look at her, so he reminded himself that he shouldn't. One glimpse of those sparkling green eyes or those dimples in her cheeks and his heart would turn completely to mush.

"Three weeks, Arthur," Merry posed.

"At least four," Arthur returned. "What goes up for Christmas must come down after."

"Okay, four. And it's not even full time. I can still work part time here."

"If he even offers it. I say you're outta your league, Merry."

"Christmas *is* my league!" Merry enthused.

Finally, Arthur stopped what he was doing. He hazarded a glance in Merry's general direction, fighting to maintain his resolve. He pointed out to the floor of his establishment. In an instant, he felt his ears turn scarlet, the way they always did whenever he got worked up over anything.

"Ever see them rich people in this diner?" he spat out. "No. They're uptown in cafés and fancy schmancy restaurants charging more than you and me make all day."

"Artie, this is my time," Merry implored. "I know it. This is my Christmas. So, would you please just roll with me on this?"

Arthur mulled it over, hesitantly. He ran a tired hand through his thinning hair as Kiki stepped into the fray. He saw Kiki plant herself, put her hands on her hips, and burn him with the kind of look that only Kiki could give.

"You don't let Merry do this, then I quit," Kiki vowed. "Either way you're way up a holiday creek."

Arthur knew when he was outgunned. Merry had always been a good waitress, but Kiki was a great one. She'd been serving the Downtown Diner's customers since the very beginning. He couldn't afford to lose Kiki, not in this economy, and certainly not during the upcoming holiday rush. "All right, I give. Fine," Arthur conceded. "So, get out there and get cracking!"

Merry gave Arthur an exuberant kiss on the cheek and scurried back out toward the restaurant's service floor.

Arthur sighed dejectedly as she left. Everything in him wanted to read something more than the flush of excitement into Merry's burst of affection, though he knew deep down that he shouldn't.

Kiki softened. "Can't lose what you don't have."

Arthur watched Merry from the kitchen. She was already back wiping the counter, charming his customers, obviously elated about the possibilities.

"She don't have that job yet," he insisted to Kiki. "Think I want to see her crushed? Best she face up and get on with it."

Kiki shook her head with a grin. She could reach him like no one else could.

"Artie, you're something," she teased. "You think you're some kind of Oprah, don't you? Well, maybe folks'll start listening to all them pearls when you start listening to yourself."

♥   ♥   ♥

Catherine searched her purse as she exited Strong Bank & Trust with Daniel. She enjoyed having him back on her arm. It wasn't that she'd felt threatened in any way when she'd seen him step out for coffee with Merry. From her vantage point at the top of the mezzanine stairs, Merry had seemed waifish at best. Her uniform and worn sensible shoes had done absolutely nothing for her appearance.

Just as soon as he'd returned, Daniel had been careful to explain to her that Merry had just wanted to talk to him about the Christmas Coordinator position, and that qualifications hadn't so much been her strong suit.

It was a mercy interview, Catherine intuited. Even if it hadn't been, she couldn't imagine that there would be a problem. Still, something inside her hoped Daniel would go another way.

Catherine fished a ticket stub out of her bag. She handed it to the valet, then turned to Daniel. "If you're looking for someone more seasoned to coordinate, I have a great service I've used. They're very professional," she promised. "They'd take care of everything, first class all the way."

"Thanks, but...I'm still mulling it over," Daniel replied. "She's a little green, but...it might work out with the kids. I don't know."

Catherine was pleased to have come prepared. She went back into her designer clutch and found a business card. She extended it to Daniel as offhandedly as she could. "Well, here's the service, in case. Ask for Philippe. Tell him you're with me and he'll clear his calendar."

Daniel accepted the card with a smile. "I like the sound of that—saying I'm with you." He put his arm around her waist, making her glad she'd worked so hard on it with her trainer.

"Do you, now?" she coyly replied.

Daniel maintained a pleasant, nonchalant air. "Perhaps it's no surprise, but...I do have intentions toward you, Catherine."

Catherine took it in, making her designs upon him every bit as clear. "Good to know."

♥   ♥   ♥

It had been easy for Merry to wait through the night. A man like Daniel wouldn't be rash, she reasoned. He would probably sleep on the decision. Merry had said her prayers. She'd nodded off, blissful at the events of the day. For hours she'd slept soundly, that was, until she heard the slap of Mr. Grabinski's newspaper being flung onto the stoop at 4:30 a.m.

For a long while, Merry resisted crawling out from beneath the covers. She tried to have faith that the best would come to be. But by five, she found herself padding down the stairs of the walk-up, dressed in her terry robe and slippers.

Carefully, Merry pulled out the classifieds and stood under the yellowed lantern by the door. She turned the pages and scanned the Help Wanted ads meticulously, searching for any sign of whether or not Daniel had gone ahead and posted his ad after meeting her.

There was nothing. Merry breathed a relieved sigh.

By the time Merry got to the Downtown Diner later that morning, Skeeter was standing by the newspaper machine, counting what little change had been tossed into his cup. She liked the way his weathered face brightened whenever he saw her round the corner with a brown bag in her hand. Merry figured it was an even trade for the fact that Arthur always kept her fed when things slowed down at the diner. So, as often as she could, she brought a bag lunch for Skeeter. Inside, there would be his favorite tuna sandwich and some of those cheesy puffs that made his chocolate-brown fingers turn orange. A juice box would wash it all down to soothe his growling stomach.

"Hi, ya, Skeeter, " Merry grinned. She handed him the sack. "God bless you."

"He does," Skeeter nodded. "Thank you, Sweetheart."

As Merry entered the diner's door, a little bell rang. A yellowed plastic Santa at the register leaned back mechanically, then bobbed up and down with a raspy sort of *ho-ho-ho*. She shot a look at Arthur.

Arthur glanced up from the grill. A sheepish curl formed on his lips. "Yeah, I figured it was time to coordinate a little Christmas around here, too."

Relieved not to have to broach the subject, Merry seized the opportunity. "Did he call yet?"

"Nope," Arthur replied. "But we got a bus load of blue hairs coming for a birthday party. So, get hopping, Hopper."

Merry kicked into gear. "Be right back," she promised before she spun right into Kiki, whose empty tray went flying. "Sorry!" she called, retrieving Kiki's tray.

Arthur opened his mouth to comment, but Kiki intervened. "You hush, now."

Arthur recoiled. "Who you telling—"

"Shoosh," Kiki ordered as she accepted the tray back from Merry. "Just you think about it first with your smart self. What would Oprah do?"

It had been a long day for Merry. There had been no call about the Christmas Coordinator job, even a quick buzz just to check Arthur as a reference. Arthur hadn't mentioned it. He didn't have to. With each passing hour, it had become harder for Merry not to give into disappointment.

The diner was closed for the night. Business hours were over. Still, Merry dove to answer when the phone rang.

"Arthur's." Once again, Merry's face fell. "No, Arthur's as in the Downtown Diner...Okay, bye." Merry sighed as she hung up, with a sheepish glance toward Arthur.

"You always got your job here," Arthur reminded.

"Thanks. You know, just because I wanted that temp job doesn't mean I don't appreciate what I've got."

Suddenly, the phone rang again. Merry started for it, but Arthur put up a hand to stop her. He picked it up himself.

"Arthur's...Yeah, you got him."

Merry caught her breath. Her fading ember of hope burst back into flame.

Arthur shooed Merry away. "Yeah, she told me you might call."

Arthur's look said it all. It was the call Merry had been waiting for all day.

"She's a good girl," Arthur continued. "Hate to give her up, but...Couldn't do better if you ask me...Well, hang on. Lemme check." Arthur put the phone on hold and turned to Merry. "Mr. Moneybags wants to know if I can spare you, as soon as tomorrow."

Merry silently pleaded.

"How am I supposed to say no to you?" Arthur groused.

True to her name, Merry hopped up and down. "Oh, thank you! Thank you!"

"All right, already," he bellowed. "So, pick up the phone, before I come to my senses."

SUSAN ROHRER

There were times in Merry's life when she could hardly imagine that she was awake, that a turn life had taken really was happening. That's how it was for Merry the next morning. She looked around, wanting to drink in every detail of it.

The early December air was crisp; the sky was a brilliant blue. It offset stately elms lining an affluent street Merry had never even dreamed to explore. Iron fences led to tony brownstones, each with its own stairway, leading up to individual doorways. *Here I am*, she thought, marveling that it was true. She glanced heavenward with a smile, knowing it was the answer to her prayer.

As she passed each residence, Merry checked addresses against a slip of paper in her hand. Finding the matching house number, she stopped and looked up, dwarfed by a four-story townhouse.

Merry took hold of the rail and climbed the stairs. She reached for a brass knocker just as the over-sized door flew open and nine year-old Ollie Bell blew by her, then bounded down the stairs and sprinted for the arriving school bus.

"Hi!" Merry called after him.

Ollie glanced back with a wave, "Hi, bye, whoever you are!"

Next out the door was Ollie's older sister, Tara. One of the two, Merry surmised. Tara glided out, put together more like a model from a fashion magazine than a teenager headed for school.

"Pardon moi," Tara said, scooting by Merry.

"Gotta be Tara," Merry intuited, just as her sister, Hayden ambled out in grungy contrast, zipping her laptop into her pack.

"Yeah, so how'd you tell the difference?" Hayden asked.

"Uh... The computer?"

Apparently, Hayden didn't buy it. "What, not my chichi fashion sense?"

Tara called back to her twin impatiently, "Will you shake it, Hayden?"

Hayden tromped down the steps, calling to Tara sardonically. "Yeah, wouldn't want to miss a second of walking in your shadow."

Merry grinned, happy to think that the adventure of this job was already starting. She spun around to the door, inadvertently crashing into Daniel. Again. The proximity was a bit awkward, but she was at least glad that she didn't have coffee to spill on him this time.

"Good morning, Merry," he said.

"Oh! Hi. I met the kids. Sort of."

Daniel headed down the steps. "I'm off, too, but stop by the bank before lunch and I'll get you set with the Christmas account. Mom is in the kitchen, she'll show you around."

Merry watched Daniel as he opened the door of his Range Rover, parked out front.

"Thank you!" she called. "You won't be sorry you gave me this chance."

"Certainly hope not," Daniel smiled as he climbed into the car. The door closed with the solid ca-thunk of a posh family vehicle, worlds apart from Merry's repossessed Bug. In fact, Merry noticed that the whole street was lined with shiny, new luxury cars. It made her realize the advantage of having had to walk a few blocks from the El's stop, since her faded, forty year-old car would have seemed so completely incongruous.

Turning, Merry stepped into the handsome residence and closed the door. Knowing there was only one first time for everything, she savored each step of the experience. Taking it all in, she wandered through the foyer and into the tastefully appointed living room. There was a handsome leather chair and ottoman that she supposed Mr. Bell frequented. Cushy sofa pillows accented the colors in an Oriental carpet that was almost the size of her whole studio apartment.

Though there was no escaping the awe Merry felt of what wealth can provide, the personal touches were what captured her attention most. There on an end table was a family photo. She could tell it had been taken years ago, both from the way the kids had all grown since and the fact that a comely brunette stood beside Mr. Bell, his arm around her shoulders.

Merry lifted the frame for a closer look, and the surrounding photos dominoed, clattering onto the tabletop. Merry did her best to quickly regroup as Daniel's mother, Joan, entered from the kitchen, drying her hands with a tea towel.

"Oops. Sorry," Merry said, her face reddening.

Joan smiled warmly. "No worries. I always do the same thing myself. I think it's rigged that way." Joan stepped in to help Merry with the photos, not an ounce of pretense in her voice.

"That's his wife?" Merry inquired. "I mean, it was?"

Joan gazed at the photo fondly. "Amanda, yes. Lovely, wasn't she?"

Merry nodded as Joan set the photo back into its place.

"I'm Joan. Mother, slash grandmother, slash chief cook and bottle-washer." Joan offered her hand, which Merry readily shook.

"I'm Merry. M-E-R-R-Y."

"Yes, Daniel told me."

"Oh, Daniel," Merry repeated. "Right. I heard that was his first name."

Joan chuckled. "What, does he have you calling him Mr. Bell?"

"I just did," Merry demurred. "Out of respect and all."

"Well, out of respect for my age-sensitivity issues, do you think you could call me Joan?"

Merry smiled broadly, liking Joan immediately. She followed her on an impromptu tour of the downstairs, taking in the layout. Down the hall, Joan led Merry into a nicely furnished study.

"So, this will be your work area. By day."

Merry took in the masculinely decorated space. "Wow...very, uh, manly."

"Yes, it's Daniel's," Joan added. "Not that he's ever home to use it. Works too hard if you ask me." Joan pulled a small key ring out of a bowl on the desk. "Here's your key—door and deadbolt." She handed it to Merry. "Use line three on the phone. The phone book is in the lower left drawer. Upper right is yours for stowing Christmas secrets. The children know it's off limits, but check it mornings in case Daniel leaves a communiqué."

Merry opened the Christmas drawer. It was empty, but for a single envelope with "Miss Merry Hopper" penned on it.

Joan stepped back toward the door. "Well, I hate to abandon you, but I'd better scoot. I teach pottery at a little shop around the corner. Number two on speed dial, anytime you need me."

"Two. Got it," Merry assured. She looked around happily. "Is it way too soon to start loving this job?"

Joan smiled warmly. "I'd say you're just in time. And who knows? This could turn into quite the little sleigh ride after all."

As Joan left, an idea suddenly popped into Merry's head. She sat down in Daniel's swivel desk chair and jotted down a note: *Sleigh Ride*. Happily, Merry spun around in Daniel's chair. This, she convinced herself, was going to be good.

four

Merry sank into an overstuffed chair, across from Daniel's desk at Strong Bank & Trust, unabashedly amazed. How different it felt to be there than it had on her original visit just two days prior. She was actually getting to know someone there now, and that *someone* had hired her for the job of her dreams. It wasn't that she felt entitled to be there. In fact, she knew this job was far from what she'd ever deserved. What it felt like was that a brightly wrapped gift had dropped into her lap—straight out of heaven—and she was just starting to untie the ribbon.

Daniel drew up an expense account notebook as Merry watched, still pinching herself. Gone was the desperation of having to apply for a loan. Gone was the abject terror of not being able to pay her December rent or to put food in Rudy's belly. She was beginning to live out a Christmas miracle, and everything in her knew it.

Daniel passed a spreadsheet to Merry. She accepted it readily, doing her best not to betray the fact that it was the first one she'd ever been called upon to use. As lean as things had been, Merry knew that she could make a little go a long way, so she tried not to let all the numbers intimidate her as much as those things normally did.

"So, within this budget, you're pre-approved to sign for incremental withdrawals," Daniel explained. "Whenever you need another advance, you'll turn in the receipts from the previous one to access the next. We can arrange a deposit for anything you need to outsource."

"Outsource?" Merry asked.

"Like a caterer for Christmas dinner, or if you could throw a little party on Christmas Eve—maybe some extended family, a few friends. Mainly, it would be for the kids."

Merry nodded, jotting it all down on a notepad. "Do you know what they want?"

Daniel paused. For the first time, she saw a break in Daniel's otherwise completely professional demeanor.

"Actually, Christmas, it... Well, it was more Amanda's department," Daniel confessed. "So, hopefully you can burrow into those mysterious adolescent minds of theirs and figure it all out. Don't skimp, but don't go crazy. No cars or computers or personal TVs. The last thing I want to do is to spoil them. Just a simple, nice, old-fashioned family Christmas. Sound do-able to you?"

As Daniel handed Merry the account book, Catherine approached, impeccably dressed. Her heel clicks echoed as she crossed the marble-tiled floor. Daniel rose immediately. Merry followed suit.

Catherine looked Merry over, and then turned to Daniel. "Almost ready?"

Ever the gentleman, Daniel made introductions. "Merry, I'd like you to meet Catherine Strong."

Reflexively, Merry gawked at Catherine's last name. "Strong—you mean, as in the name of this whole bank?"

"My father," Catherine replied smoothly.

"She's on the board," Daniel interjected. "And we have a meeting across town, so—"

Merry extended her hand. "Catherine. Nice to meet you. I'm Merry. As in Christmas."

"Oh. How very...apropos," Catherine replied, exchanging a mystified glance with Daniel.

Sensing the slight, Merry took their cue. "I should go. Get started."

With a cheerful wave, Merry backed toward the door. Before she turned, she saw Catherine discreetly move a few raised fingers in return. Her brow arched with a hint of superiority that stuck in Merry's throat. Then, just as Merry reached the exit, she distinctly heard Catherine's assessment.

"She's delightful, Daniel," Catherine remarked. "Almost—I don't know—like a Dickens character, don't you think?"

Her face reddening, Merry pushed through the revolving door. It wasn't Catherine's tone that had bothered her, or even the first part of what she had said. It was that dismissive sort of put-down at the end.

As Merry spun outside and hurried away, something about those final words of Catherine's rang in her ears. They taunted her all the way down the block till she disappeared around the corner. They mocked her about her clothes and her hair and her childlike effervescence.

Safely out of sight, Merry stopped. She did her best to pluck out the barb and nurse her wounded pride. It was ironic, she told herself. She had long identified with the orphans of Dickens; she'd read his books cover to cover.

Chin up, she thought. She was who she was, and that was that. Nothing was going to steal the joy of her day. Though no one was there to see or hear it, Merry willed herself to throw her shoulders back and smile. She nodded, and then said what she needed to say. "Thank you, Catherine. I'll consider that a compliment."

Back at the Bell's townhouse, Merry spread out craft supplies on the kitchen table. Happily, she organized an eclectic assortment of colorfully patterned dinnerware, ribbons, beads, wire, bells, doodads, and odd recyclables over a protective covering of newsprint. Merry had always loved creating things. She enjoyed the adventure that making something out of what seemed like nothing could be. Her eyes shining, she scanned the diverse array. Never before had she had such nice materials, nor so many shimmering possibilities.

Ollie loped in through the back door. He ditched his backpack on the counter and made a beeline straight for the cookie jar. "Hi, again, whoever you are," he chirped.

Merry looked up from her work. Something in Ollie's easy acceptance of her presence made her begin to feel at home. "Hi, again."

Ollie looked at her quizzically. "Are you that Merry Christmas person?"

"Yup," Merry nodded. "Just getting going here."

Ollie eyed the table. "What's all that stuff?"

"For ornaments. For the tree."

"Why don't you just buy some at the store?" Ollie asked, stuffing a chocolate chip cookie into his mouth.

"More fun to make them," Merry countered. "That way, it's a memory you'll be hanging. Wanna help?"

Ollie crinkled his nose at the prospect. "Looks like it's for girls."

Merry sighed cheerily. "Well, your sisters, they said they had homework. So, the opportunity is wide open."

Ollie shook his head warily as he retrieved his backpack. "I think I might have homework, too."

"Okay," Merry accepted, going on with her work. Then, with a nonchalant nod to the pile of dinnerware, she added, "But you'd get to break stuff."

Not long later, a colorful plate smashed into an outdoor fireplace in the Bell's backyard. Merry turned to Ollie, admiring his toss. "Oooh, good one. Why don't you try a couple of these teacups?"

Wearing an oddly protective snorkeling mask and oven mitts, Ollie grabbed the cups and sent them sailing into the barbeque where they shattered into pieces. "Smithereens!" he shouted gleefully.

Merry climbed the stairs and approached the bedroom the Bell girls shared. The twins hadn't come to her, so she would try going to them. As she reached the doorway, Merry saw Tara first. She was rifling impatiently through her closet. Hayden was across the room, sitting on her bed with her laptop and books, apparently trying to make a dent in her homework.

"This is hopeless," Tara moped. "He's seen every single permutation of every last piece I've got."

"You're welcome to my wardrobe," Hayden offered flatly.

"Funny," Tara groaned.

It felt kind of odd to Merry that the girls weren't acknowledging her presence. She reminded herself that it would be more challenging to break the ice with them than it had been with Ollie. She gave the doorjamb a light rap. "Got a sec?"

Tara nodded acceptingly. She waved at Merry to come in, a conniving glint in her eyes. "So...since you're the one doing the whole Christmas thing—"

Merry shrugged congenially, "Well, I kind of thought we'd all do it."

Tara marched straight to her desk and grabbed a piece of paper. "Well, anyway, you'll be happy to know I've already done my part."

Hayden barely looked up to add, "Yeah, she's been making her list and checking it twice ever since Dad said we could have Christmas."

"That's great," Merry said. "I was going to ask you to make lists."

"Yeah, I'll get right on that," Hayden replied, her tone dripping with cynicism.

Undaunted, Tara handed Merry a lengthy list. Impressed, Merry scanned it.

"My favorite boutiques, my color palette and sizes," Tara explained. "Daddy may resist the Beemer, but still try. Not like he can't afford it."

Merry's eyes widened. Though taken aback by the list's contents, she knew she wanted to get off on the right foot with Tara. "This is some list. Very... complete."

Hayden chortled. "Yeah, she's actually glad to be Christmassing again. Amazing we have the same DNA."

Tara whirled toward her twin. "I'm just trying to be supportive. Not everyone has to be all grinch-o-rama like you."

Undaunted, Hayden ripped off a blank piece of notebook paper and held it up. "Yeah. Here's my list. I don't want anything."

Desperate to diffuse the situation, Merry stepped closer. "Oh, you know what? I'm sorry. See, I was hoping you'd each make a list of what you want to get for everybody else. Not even stuff to buy necessarily. Just things you really want for each other."

"Don't even get me started on that," Hayden replied.

Tara studied Merry, puzzled. "Wait. These lists, they're...she's... That's what we're going to get?"

"The lists would be of what you're going to give," Merry clarified.

Tara wrinkled her brow. Hayden stifled a giggle. Finally, Tara snatched the lists from Merry. Then, ceremoniously, Tara gave her own laundry list of desired gifts to Hayden and grabbed Hayden's blank list for herself. "Done!" Tara pronounced as she strode out victoriously.

Left alone with Hayden, Merry wasn't sure what to do. Though she'd never had a family of her own, she knew what sibling rivalry could be like from her youth spent with other kids in orphanages and foster care. At a loss for what to say, Merry sent up a silent plea for help.

Hayden perused Tara's list. She rolled her eyes, crumpled it up and tossed it into her wastebasket. She plopped back down on her bed and resumed her studies as if Merry wasn't even there.

Merry was used to feeling invisible. She'd felt that way most of her life. But this wasn't about how Merry felt and she knew it. It was about Hayden. Merry took a deep breath, realizing that they were nothing alike. She searched her mind for common ground, any way into Hayden's locked up heart.

Merry tentatively ambled into the room. "I almost had a sister once. I always wanted one," she ventured.

"Want mine?" Hayden shot back, never even looking up from her work.

"I wish it were that easy."

Hayden finally looked at Merry. "Who says it's easy having one? Especially if I'm supposed to want to give her something that she doesn't already have. She's more popular. She's got a boyfriend. She's prettier."

Seeing a crack in Hayden's armor, Merry risked perching on the end of her bed. "Hayden, why do you... I mean, you're both beautiful. You're twins."

Hayden shook her head. "And in every set there's an Alpha. You're looking at the uncontested Beta, here."

Merry sat quietly for a moment, understanding what it was like to be passed over all too well. "Not so big on Christmas, huh?"

At the mention of the season, Hayden looked sadly peeved. "Look. Even if I wanted to rally around the Christmas tree—which I so completely don't—I've still got nothing for Tara. Nothing she'd want."

Hayden broke eye contact with Merry. She picked up a pencil and seemed only to pretend to resume her homework.

Merry read Hayden's signal. Not wanting to press too far too soon, she rose from the bed. "You seem really smart, Hayden. Smarter than I ever was. As far as what Tara might like you to give her this Christmas goes, well...you'll think of something."

Merry wandered away, down the upstairs hallway. She gazed at the family photos along the wall. Indeed, it was easy to tell Tara from Hayden in the pictures. They'd been dressed alike as babies, and similarly in childhood shots, as many young twins are. But clearly, as the girls had grown into their teens, their differences had emerged. From the first of the photos where their mother was absent, Tara was completely put together in every picture, while Hayden looked deliberately disheveled.

Reaching the hall bathroom, Merry noticed Tara inside, working on her hair. It had already been well coifed, but Tara still busied herself, styling it to look even better. Merry stopped in the doorway. "You have a date?"

Tara twisted a strand and secured it into an interesting clip. "After dinner. To study."

Merry ventured closer. "That's cute. Wish I could get my hair to do stuff like that."

"I got Mom's hair," Tara responded. "Good thing. Dad's is kind of gnarly."

Merry thought about her own gene pool. It was like diving into one of those murky green swimming holes where you had no idea what was beneath the surface, let alone who had taken a dip in it, or what they might have left in the water. Where she came from wasn't anything Merry talked about much, but something inside told her that she should. "I don't know whose hair I got. Never saw either one of my parents."

Tara stopped what she was doing and turned to Merry. "No way."

Merry confirmed it with a nod. "Way. Never even knew their names."

"That must be kind of weird," Tara said. "So, who named you?"

"Social Services," Merry answered. "Somebody found me, brand spanking newborn on the church steps Christmas morning. That's why they called me Merry. My last name, Hopper—they said that was because I was left there in this coal hopper thing and...I guess it fit."

Something in Tara seemed to soften, at least momentarily. "Yeah, it fits. It does."

Noticing the blank list Tara had taken from Hayden on the counter, Merry picked it up. "You were just torturing Hayden with this, right? You don't really want to give her a big old nothing for Christmas, do you?"

Tara's face fell a bit. "Not like she wants anything from me."

"Oh, I don't know," Merry encouraged. "She might."

Tara looked skeptical. "Like what? Did she say something?"

Merry shook her head. "No, no. And I can't really put my finger on it yet, but...maybe you will. Maybe you'll surprise her."

It took a moment or two, but Merry could tell that Tara's wheels had begun to turn. "Maybe," she echoed. Tara took the blank paper, left the bathroom and headed down the stairs toward the kitchen.

It was just a baby step, but Merry knew it was progress, good progress for a first day. Merry leaned against the doorjamb, savoring the small victory. She mouthed a happy *thanks* and breathed a satisfied sigh.

♥ ♥ ♥

Downstairs, Joan unloaded groceries as Tara passed through. "Honey, could you set the table?"

"Sure," Tara agreed. "Gramma, what do you think of Merry?"

Joan piled fresh-washed cherries in a bowl on the counter. It wasn't often that her grandchildren asked her opinion, so she enjoyed the fact that Tara had as she mulled over her first impressions. "I like her. Just something about her."

Tara opened the cupboard door. "Yeah. Too bad Dad's so into that Catherine person," she sighed, finding only empty shelves in front of her. "So, where are all the plates?"

"Try the dishwasher, dear," Joan answered.

Suddenly, Ollie's triumphant voice rang out from the backyard. "Smithereens!"

Joan recognized the distinct crash of breaking china that followed. In a flash, Joan was out the back door, just in time to see Ollie raise an ornate china platter high above his head, as if to acknowledge the cheers of an imaginary throng. He whirled it around like a discus thrower. "Ho, ho—"

Recognizing the platter, Joan shouted in horror. "No! Ollie, don't!"

"—ho!" Ollie cried as he released the platter and sent it soaring into the brick fireplace, dashing it to pieces.

Tara emerged, agape at the sight. "You are so getting coal for Christmas."

Joan hurried down the stairs. "Ollie, what are you doing?! That's the good family china!"

Ollie turned, grinning to beat the band. "It's okay, Gramma. Merry said so," he exuded. "I'm making memories. For Christmas!"

five

❧ ♥ ❧

Tara and Hayden cleared the Bell's dinner table as Merry sat guiltily with Ollie on the living room sofa. Tara lingered, a look of concern on her face, as her father silently paced in front of the culprits.

Merry kicked herself. The thrill ride of her first day had come to a screeching halt. Her mind whirled. Why hadn't she been clearer with Ollie? Though she feared it would get her fired, Merry knew what she had to say. Her heart pounding, she prodded herself to open her mouth and speak. Finally, the fearsome words that she knew could end it all came out. "It was all my fault. Really, Mr. Bell."

Daniel studied Merry, and then turned to his young son. "Ollie, did you not know that was the good family china?"

"She said it was okay!" Ollie protested.

"I did, Sir. In a way," Merry admitted.

"Please, do not call me *Sir*," Daniel blustered. "And I assume you have an explanation why you're encouraging my son to engage in vandalism?"

"It was a mix up," Merry explained. "I'd bought these thrift store dishes. I got them to break and make ornaments from the pieces. Then, I went up to talk to the girls and—"

Daniel cut her off. "Yes. So they tell me," he said. He turned to his son. "Ollie, would you go do your homework?"

Ollie glanced at Merry, his brow knit with worry. "But what's going to happen to—"

Daniel quickly gestured to the stairway. "Now, Oliver. I'll be up in a bit." Ollie obediently headed up the steps. Next, Daniel pivoted to address his eavesdropping daughters. "Girls, I believe your grandmother could use your help in the kitchen."

As the twins reluctantly disappeared, Merry stood, imploring, "Please. Take the price of the china out of my pay."

"And just how do I dock you for the sentimental value of it?" Daniel countered. "That platter was an heirloom. From their mother's side. Let alone worth a small fortune."

"And can I tell you how completely awful I feel about that?" Merry rued.

Daniel kept pacing, then abruptly he stopped. He turned back to Merry, weary and forlorned. "You promised me the perfect Christmas."

"I did," Merry replied. "But Mr. Bell...perfect doesn't mean everything goes exactly right. That kind of perfect, it's pretty much forgettable, I think. But when something goes wrong—well, that really is the kind of thing you hang your memories on."

The tiniest flicker of a change on Daniel's face told Merry that somehow, she was starting to get through to him. She knew that she was still a long way from out of the woods, but it encouraged her to continue. "Years from now, think of it," she said. "Ollie will be putting those ornaments on his own tree. Can't you just hear him laughing, telling your grandkids the story?"

Daniel crinkled his lips, softening ever so slightly. "I suppose you could spin it that way. But what's this with these lists? The girls don't want to do it. At least, Hayden doesn't."

"You said you wanted a family Christmas," Merry reminded.

"Which I expected you to handle."

SUSAN ROHRER

Merry braved stepping closer to Daniel. She kept her voice calm and quiet enough so as not to be overheard by the twins she presumed might be listening in, just past the kitchen door. "That's why I'm trying to get them to be part of it. If I just think it up, buy it up, put it up, and wrap it up myself, how special would that be?"

Daniel sat tiredly, his tone changing. He scratched the back of his head. "You sound like Amanda. Next thing, you'll tell me I work too much."

Merry sat back down beside him. "Do you?"

"Maybe," Daniel replied. "It's not like it's been easy. Raising them alone. Trying to get them past what I—maybe not get them past it. That's not the right word. It's not like I want them to forget, but... Why am I telling you this?"

Merry smiled softly, understanding. "Maybe you sense that I care to hear it. Because I do. Care."

Daniel studied Merry. "You do. Really?"

"Yeah," she answered. A moment of silence passed between them, before Merry finally broke it. "Can I...ask you something?"

"Sure," Daniel agreed.

Merry looked Daniel straight in the eyes. It was a gaze that said she wasn't going to let this go. "What do you want this Christmas?"

Daniel didn't answer at first. It was a loaded question for him, Merry realized. *I'm his employee*, she thought. He was under no obligation to answer her, she knew, yet something in the moment had seemed to disarm him completely.

"I want..." Daniel started. "It's not much really, but then again, it's..." Daniel paused again. "I want to see my family happy again. I'd like to go back to church together. We haven't been much since Amanda's memorial—my fault really—and I don't know. Maybe Christmas morning would be a good start. I do want to make some new memories...not to replace the old ones, but to somehow..."

"...take the broken pieces and make something beautiful with them?"

Daniel took awhile to consider Merry's response. He looked at her, what almost seemed to be through her, for the longest of times. Finally, he spoke. "You're easily underestimated, aren't you?"

Merry nodded self-deprecatingly. "I've been told I make a better second impression. That is, if I get a chance to make a second impression?"

Time stood still. At least it seemed to as Daniel studied Merry. Clearly, she thought, he had fully intended to fire her on the spot, but thank heaven, something was making him hesitate.

"Let's see what the week brings," he concluded.

♥   ♥   ♥

When Daniel ambled in to check on him, Ollie was sprawled on his stomach on his bedroom floor, doing his math homework. "There's always that desk I got you."

Ollie hardly looked up at his dad. "I can work stuff out better here."

It wasn't often that Daniel Bell sat cross-legged on the floor, but on this particular night, that's exactly what he decided to do. As soon as he got down to his son's level, he was glad he'd gone to the trouble. He noticed Ollie's quivering lip, but decided not to make anything of it. "So... What do you have going there?"

"Long division," Ollie muttered gloomily. "Mrs. Finkelston says it's useful in every day life."

Daniel leaned back quizzically. "You have Mrs. Finkelston? I had her. What, is she ninety?"

Ollie pushed his math aside and sat up. Crocodile tears rolled down his cheeks, streaking through the dirt of his ill-fated, heirloom-breaking deed.

Daniel opened his arms and drew his son close for a very welcomed embrace. "I'm sorry I broke your family china," Ollie blubbered.

"It's okay," Daniel assured. "And it's not really my family china. It was ours. Just something your mom's family has passed down for the past few hundred years." Daniel broke the embrace. He checked around, then signaled Ollie closer and whispered conspiratorially. "Want to know a secret?"

Ollie wiped his nose on his sleeve, clearly intrigued.

Daniel leaned toward him. "I always kind of hated that platter."

Ollie's eyes widened. "You did?"

Daniel sat back. "Yeah. I always thought it was kind of snooty and girlie. Not a guy's kind of plate, you know? Guys like us, we don't go for that stuff. Your mom wasn't so crazy about it, either. But we were stuck with it—it being in the family that long—so actually, you kind of did me a favor."

A crooked little smirk returned to Ollie's lips. "I did?"

"Did yourself one, too. Because guess who would have gotten it next." Daniel circled a finger toward Ollie.

Ollie exhaled dramatically. "That was a close one."

"Yeah, scary close," Daniel agreed. "You know, Merry. She seems to think we should make these lists, so... What do you really want for Christmas?"

Ollie didn't miss a beat. "A worm farm," he repeated.

Daniel eyed his son, amused. "Still with the worm farm, huh?"

Ollie nodded decisively.

"Worms, they don't do much, you know," Daniel went on. "Not so big on thrills and chills. Can't race 'em or goof with 'em. Just kind of hang out there under the dirt."

Ollie's shoulders went up in a little shrug. "Marty Ruppick has one," he pointed out. "Marty grows lots and lots of worms. Then his dad takes him fishing."

There it was.

It was so simple that Daniel wondered why he hadn't put it together before. It wasn't so much the worms Ollie wanted, Daniel realized. What Ollie wanted most for Christmas was his time.

Long after his children had gone to bed, Daniel sat in his study, deep in thought. Nothing about this roller coaster ride of a day had gone like he had supposed. He finished off a short note and slipped it into the Christmas drawer, knowing Merry would find it in the morning.

♥   ♥   ♥

Even after finishing up the late shift at the Downtown Diner, there was a spring in Merry's step as she walked with Kiki toward the stop where they would catch the El to their respective homes. Despite the disastrous heirloom platter incident, Merry was quietly exuberant. For Arthur's sake, Merry hadn't said much about her job with the Bells. She'd only spoken about it in the most general of terms. Still, Merry felt Kiki studying her, the way Kiki did whenever she'd figured out that something intriguing was afoot.

"So, gimme the real skinny on this Christmas gig," Kiki probed.

Merry did her best to feign nonchalance. "You heard what I told Arthur."

"Yeah, I heard you dancing 'round the doo-doo for him, but this is me. Kiki. So, let's have it straight now."

Merry cocked her head with a smile. She lit up from inside. "Almost got fired today."

"So, why you glowing like a Tiki torch?"

Though Merry did her best to downplay her excitement, it still kept bubbling through. Still, she did her best not to say too much. "No, it was just...he has this cute way of being all boss-man, but underneath, I get these little glimmers that he's... It was good, that's all."

Kiki clasped her hands and raised them toward the heavens. "Precious Lord, help us!" Then turning back to Merry, she nailed what even Merry hadn't realized. "You jazzin' on that man!"

Merry sputtered, taken completely off-guard. "No, no, I mean, he is—"

"I know sparks when I see 'em," Kiki crowed, "and Honeypot, you about to set this here track on fire."

Merry felt her face turn crimson. She covered it with her hands. "Augghh! No, no, no. You know what? I can't even go there."

"Well, that kit's already caboodled."

Merry grabbed Kiki's arm in desperation. "It is not! It can't be. Okay, okay. Maybe it is. But it's just in my head."

"Oh, it's on your face, too," Kiki hooted.

Mortified, Merry stopped in her tracks. "Is it that obvious? What if he can tell?"

Kiki shook it off. "Naw, Baby. Men don't see that inside stuff. That's why God made women."

♥   ♥   ♥

Hours later, all was quiet at the Bell household. Ollie checked the clock in his father's study. It read 2:10 a.m. Painstakingly, Ollie tiptoed to his dad's desk.

He knew he wasn't allowed up at that hour, much less to prowl his dad's study, but curiosity over just what he'd be getting for Christmas had gotten the better of him.

Reaching his father's desk, Ollie eyed the forbidden fruit: the mysteriously taboo Christmas drawer, the one he knew was completely off limits. Unable to resist, Ollie carefully slid the drawer open. Suddenly, the lamp flipped on, illuminating the room. Ollie startled to see Tara.

"Augh!"

Tara padded over quickly, her finger to her lips. "Shhhhh!"

His little heart pounding, Ollie whispered emphatically. "You shush! What are you doing here?"

"Same as you, apparently," Tara retorted.

Ollie looked back quizzically. "Seeing what I'm getting for Christmas?"

Tara pushed Ollie aside, made a beeline for the open Christmas drawer, and removed her father's note to Merry. "Yeah, I'm really itching for a worm farm." Tara opened the envelope, pulled the note out, and read.

Ollie crowded in to see. "What's it say?"

Turning the note away from her brother, Tara quietly read its text:

Merry,

I hope you'll forgive my overreaction. Please continue to follow your heart. I can see you have a good one. And the more I think of it, the more I realize just how much I need you.

Daniel

Ollie's tired eyes widened. "Is that like a love letter?"

"No, dopey," Tara explained. "He's just apologizing for flipping out over the whole china debacle. He's just—" Tara interrupted herself, a sly expression forming. "You know...with just a little help, it could be..."

Tara grabbed her dad's pen, the same one he'd used to write the note. Carefully mimicking his handwriting, Tara inserted a *"Love,"* before her father's signature.

Ollie watched, agape. "Love, Daniel? I'm telling." Ollie started to leave, but Tara firmly yanked him back.

"You tell and I tell you were down here," Tara threatened. "Besides. Maybe if we do a little something to encourage him to like Merry, he might forget all about Miss Boring Face. It could be our gift to him, a secret. You like Merry, right?"

Ollie nodded. "Yeah, so..."

Tara slipped the note back into place in the drawer. "So, pinkie swear," she said, extending her little finger.

Never before had Tara offered to share such a confidence with Ollie. It felt good to him, like he was included in her life in a whole new way. "Our Christmas present to him, together?" he queried.

Tara nodded in affirmation, waiting for his agreement. Ollie hooked his pinkie to his sister's with a mischievous grin, sealing their holiday pact.

six

❧ ♥ ❧

Merry scurried into Daniel's study. Though she'd worked hard and late the day before, she'd awakened at dawn, invigorated by the second chance she'd been given. Her mind brimming with ideas, Merry pulled off her coat and draped it on the back of Daniel's desk chair. Dutifully, she slid open the Christmas drawer to check for instructions.

Reflexively, Merry tingled all over. Whereas she'd expected a simple list, instead there was a nice note card with just her first name written on the envelope.

Merry pulled out Daniel's note and read. That he'd told her he was sorry said a lot to her, but it meant all the more that he had gone on to affirm the goodness of her heart and to say that he needed her. It was hard for Merry to imagine, but there it was, written in his hand. Yes. He actually acknowledged that he needed her. Merry had felt many things in her life, but needed hadn't really been one of them. She had felt extraneous, overlooked, even needy. But being needed was an entirely new sensation. *"I need you,"* she read aloud, taking in the sound of it.

Suddenly, Merry noticed how the note had been signed. "Oh," she gasped. *"Love, Daniel...?"* Merry's hand flew to her mouth as she examined Daniel's signature. She had sensed that their conversation the night before had been something of a breakthrough. She knew he had lit a spark in her, but what she hadn't dared dream to consider was the possibility that the feeling could have been mutual.

Each time Merry had entered Strong Bank & Trust, it had felt different, but this fourth time had been the most strangely wonderful of all. *How had this all come to be*, she mused. As she sat waiting for Daniel to check her receipts, she replayed the events of the previous days, savoring every detail, leading up to the note signed *Love, Daniel*. It hardly seemed real to her, but there he was, receptively cordial, light years out of her league according to Arthur and yet, it was his affectionately signed card she prized in her pocket.

As Daniel counted out Merry's cash advance, she took in his darkly handsome features with freshly stirred interest. He had a very strong jaw and the tiniest bit of gray just at the top of his sideburns. She enjoyed the sound of his voice.

"Everything appears to be in order," Daniel said, maintaining his professional air. Then, studying her demeanor, he added, "You all right today?"

Merry smiled demurely. "Fine, it's just, I got your note and I...I was kind of surprised. Good surprised. Guess I'm not used to hearing—er—I should say *reading* that kind of thing. And I know I'm like six shades of red," she added, failing to fight the blush rising to her cheeks.

Daniel took on an engagingly familiar tone. He leaned across the desk and lowered his voice to a confidential level. "To tell the truth, I did a little soul-searching after you left last night and—I didn't mean to embarrass you, but it's what I was honestly feeling. And I signed it the way I did because, well...I was hoping you'd start calling me Daniel."

Merry smiled warmly, interpreting what Daniel spoke in light of his note. His words did nothing but confirm the unimaginable. *He really is interested in me*, she thought. "It actually meant a lot that you signed it like that. I guess we're both kind of seeing how it goes, but...I'm starting to think... Let's just say that I could get used to calling you Daniel."

"Good, then," Daniel replied as he handed Merry the cash and the receipt book. He watched as she signed for both.

"And I'll do better today, on the job," Merry promised.

"You did well yesterday," Daniel reassured. "I guess for some reason I just didn't see it at first."

"Well, you know what they say," Merry replied, remembering Kiki's words. "That's why God made women. To see stuff."

Out of the corner of her eye, Merry noticed as Catherine emerged from the elevator and headed toward them. "Daniel. There you are," Catherine called.

"Boss's daughter again. Time to get back to business," Daniel whispered as Catherine neared. Quickly, he handed a folded piece of paper to Merry. "My Christmas list. Most of it. Can't think what to get for Catherine. Or Mother for that matter. Let me know if she drops a hint."

Catherine glided to a graceful stop at the edge of Daniel's desk. Both Daniel and Merry rose immediately. Catherine smiled ever so cordially. "Good morning. Merry, wasn't it?"

Merry steeled herself. "Yes. I was just—"

Catherine went on, not waiting for Merry to finish her sentence. "Daniel...a moment?" Daniel acquiesced, allowing Catherine to lead him away. As Merry perused Daniel's list, a puzzled expression grew on her face.

By the time Merry walked out of the bank, she was already on her cell with Kiki. Checking behind herself to be sure she wasn't being overheard, Merry confided. "So, the daughter of the president of the whole bank, she works there, and she's suddenly on his Christmas list. He signed this really sweet note to me *"Love, Daniel"* and it sure sounds like he's interested in me, so why is he asking me to buy her a gift?"

"Maybe he's a player."

Merry shook the thought off quickly. She'd fended off those types at the restaurant before and this felt completely different. "He just doesn't seem that way. I guess it's possible that I'm reading too much into what he said to me. Or maybe it's just a business gift he wants for her. I don't know."

"What kind of gift did he tell you to get?" Kiki asked. "That'd tip you."

"He didn't say," Merry responded. "I'm supposed to help him come up with ideas."

"So, how about you float out something romantic for her as a possibility. Fish around," Kiki advised.

"And if he bites—"

"If he does, okay, you got your answer," Kiki continued. "You bow out. But if he hesitates--well, then Girl, you might just have yourself one high-class nibble."

♥ ♥ ♥

Upstairs in the privacy of her conspicuously emptied corner office, Catherine pulled Daniel inside. Though she'd convinced herself that Merry was far from Daniel's type, something in her had still knotted up at the sight of Merry, visiting Daniel's desk once again. Catherine had never liked defending her territory. She was more of the offensive ilk. So, she closed the door, drew Daniel close, and planted a decidedly unbusiness-like kiss on him.

Daniel broke the kiss with a curious gaze around the vacant room. "Where's all your stuff?"

Catherine smiled coyly, wiping her lipstick off his lips. "Not to rush the season, but... I'm just working on an early Christmas present for you."

Daniel looked around, a stymied expression on his face. "You're leaving the company?"

"Not as long as you've got those 'intentions' on me," Catherine reminded.

Daniel nodded matter-of-factly. "There are those 'intentions' in the air."

"Wafting about."

"Yes," Daniel echoed. "They're all about the wafting."

Coyly, Catherine straightened Daniel's lapel. "And let's just say that Daddy got wind of those 'intentions' as they, ever so randomly, drifted by his soon to be retired presidential post. Let's say he would approve if I were to move just a bit down the hall, opening the possibility of redecorating here in a much more manly motif, say to accommodate the advancement of a certain attractive, extraordinarily hard-working Senior V.P."

"One with honorable intentions, no doubt," Daniel added, following her train of thought.

Catherine smiled, obviously pleased with her plan. "Then, wouldn't that make for a very Merry Christmas?"

♥ ♥ ♥

Merry spread her ornament-making supplies out on the Bell's kitchen table. Though she'd never intended to work with fine china, she could see how pieces of the broken heirloom dinnerware definitely added to the quality of the mix. As Merry sifted through for nicely patterned pieces, Joan unpacked a box of every day plates, loading them directly into the dishwasher.

"Did you buy those to replace this?" Merry asked. "I'll pay for it."

Joan brushed it off pleasantly. "No. Don't give it another thought. This is just from my apartment. I don't do anything but sleep there. And I figure this way, as long as we have something to eat on, Daniel won't run out and buy new, and it'll give me a surprise to put under the tree."

"I'd be glad to shop for you, for your grandkids. No charge," Merry offered.

"Thanks, but I've been looking forward to doing it myself," Joan replied. "Part of the fun of being a grandma, spoiling your grandkids. And this will be the first Christmas in three years I get to do that."

Merry thought about it. Joan was so easy to be with, an integral part of the Bell family. It was no wonder that she had remained such a welcomed and regular presence, long after Amanda's passing. "I can't even imagine having a mom, let alone a grandmom."

Joan stopped what she was doing. She wandered over to the kitchen table to gaze at Merry's project. "No family at all?"

Merry shook her head. "Just my boy, Rudy. My cat."

Joan picked up one of Merry's completed broken china ornaments. She complimented Merry on the way she had chosen interesting pieces, filed the sharp edges away, then fashioned wire, beads, and ribbon to set them off in such a creative way. Joan held the ornament up to the light. "Not a bad use for that old platter. Looks much better this way, if you ask me."

"You think?" Merry asked.

"I always hated that bodacious dish," Joan snickered. "Not like we ever used it. Left me completely cold. Way too la-di-dah for my taste. Don't tell Daniel."

Merry breathed a reassured sigh.

"Form follows function," Joan continued. "That's what they say in the art world. Doesn't matter how elegant it looks if it doesn't suit your family, does it?"

Merry listened intently, picking up a hint of subtext in Joan's tone. Was Joan really saying what Merry thought she was? Merry played along, testing to be sure. "So, when you're shopping. For him...for the dishes, I mean. You're saying you might not get fancy china?"

Though Joan's words remained casually discreet, her undertone continued to speak volumes. "China is, well, it's lovely to look at, to show off at society functions. Don't get me wrong; it has its place. But it's kind of fragile, high maintenance, not really built for actual family living."

Joan looked fully into Merry's face. "I'm thinking Daniel might be surprised at how much he'd like something more comfortable, still very attractive in its own way—but less fussy, more festive—like if I turned a handmade set at my pottery shop."

Merry studied Joan quizzically, surprisingly at ease. "Are we still talking about dishes?"

Joan smiled knowingly. "There's more than one kind of dish."

Merry couldn't help but press. "And you're saying...?"

Merry watched as Joan chose her words carefully. It seemed that Joan wanted to be as clear as was appropriate, without overstepping her maternal bounds.

"I'm saying," Joan confided, "What's Christmas without a secret or two between the womenfolk?"

Merry climbed the Bell's front stairs. There had been a note on the refrigerator that Tara had stayed after school for a student council function. Hayden had come straight home and wordlessly disappeared into her room.

Of all the Bell family, Merry related to Hayden the most. No matter where Merry had been as she'd bounced around the system for abandoned children, then into her adulthood—even when she'd been with other people—she'd always felt alone. Everyone else seemed to have found a sense of belonging that Merry had never had. Something in Merry longed to connect with Hayden. It was just that she had no idea how.

Merry peeked into the twins' bedroom. Hayden sat inside, clearly perplexed.

"Knock, knock," Merry started.

Hayden barely looked up. "I don't have a list for you, if that's what you want."

"No, I just..." Merry took a step inside. "Are you okay?"

"Fine."

"Because you look sort of—"

"I said I'm fine," Hayden snapped. She just sat there, sullenly staring into space.

Merry flushed. She kicked herself, realizing she'd pressed too hard too soon. Clearly Hayden didn't want her there for some reason or another. "Okay, then. I'll just... Bye." It was beyond awkward, but Merry backed out. She extracted herself the only way she could.

By the time Daniel pulled up to the garage, the sun was going down, casting a golden glow on the backyard. Merry waved cheerfully, and then went back to pruning holly boughs off of an overgrown bush. Ollie waited nearby with a large, open basket, gathering the trimmings.

Merry thought to herself how nice it was that Daniel got home at night before she had to leave. *Bankers hours*, she mused.

Daniel ambled over. He tousled Ollie's hair as he arrived, but he looked directly at Merry. He had kind eyes, she observed. He had loosened his tie.

"You don't have to do my yard work," Daniel began. "I have a man I pay."

"Just getting some holly for the mantle—Ow!" Pricked by a holly briar, Merry recoiled.

"There's big stickers on that," Ollie informed.

"Yeah," Merry agreed. "But it'll be worth it. Sometimes good stuff is that way, you know." Merry put a last sprig into Ollie's basket. "Want to run this into the living room for me?"

Ollie took the basket and went inside. Left alone with Daniel and suddenly unsure what exactly to say, Merry did what she usually did when at a loss for words. She looked for a way to busy herself. Loose holly clippings were scattered about, so she squatted to gather them. Daniel leaned down to help.

"Go all right, today?" he asked.

"Mostly. I haven't quite cracked Hayden's safe."

Daniel looked surprised. "Hayden has a safe?"

Merry smiled. "No, I'm just trying to find a way in with her."

Daniel nodded, getting it. "Well, of all of us, she's taken it the hardest. Or at least the longest." Straightening up, Daniel gestured to the holly bush nostalgically. "Amanda planted this bush, you know. She nurtured it from a seedling."

"Did she?" Merry asked, suddenly a little concerned at having taken the cuttings from it.

"She did, and just for this purpose."

Merry breathed a sigh of relief. "Good, then. That gives her a special part in this Christmas. We'll hang out the holly for her."

Daniel studied Merry intently. "How is it that you seem to know these things?"

Merry pondered it. "I don't know. Just comes to me, like it can come to anybody, I guess. Okay, put that in here." Merry extended a paper bag and Daniel deposited his clippings. "All right, you try."

"Try what?"

"Try letting a thought come to you. Not something you've thought about before. Something new. An idea."

Daniel balked a little. "I'm not so good at this. Maybe I'm too Type A, but...okay." He waited an uncomfortable moment or two. "Now, what am I supposed to do?"

"Look around for a minute. Don't stress about work or dinner or whatever. Just let something float into your head."

Clearly outside his comfort zone, Daniel still gave the notion a chance. He surveyed the yard thoughtfully, finally settling back on Merry's face.

"What do you see?" Merry asked. "Anything?"

Daniel's voice took on a softer, contemplative tone. "Light. I see light...all around you."

Merry took what he said to heart. From the way he was looking at her, she wasn't sure if his words were meant to be taken literally, but she swiveled around to refer back to the yard just in case. "I always liked the little white twinkle lights. Like stars, you know?"

Daniel nodded, turning his gaze to the yard. "Yeah. Lights would be good."

Over Daniel's shoulder, Merry saw Tara peer out at them through the blinds at the study window. Ollie appeared at her side. Suddenly, the slats were shut tight.

Stifling amusement, Merry mustered her courage. "Oh, I meant to tell you. I thought of a gift idea for Catherine. Depending on how it works with whatever your...relationship is."

Daniel mulled it over. "Yes, it's... The woman has virtually everything, so... What were you thinking?"

It was a fearsome plunge, but Merry took it, her desire to know overtaking the fright over what his answer would be. "There's this formal Ball New Year's Eve. It's a big Children's Hospital benefit."

Daniel shifted his weight and rubbed at his jaw. His expression was impossible to read. "Good thought, and I could make a donation in her name, she'd like that. But I don't actually dance."

"You didn't even dance at your wedding?" Merry probed.

Daniel smiled faintly. "That was the first and last time. Amanda coaxed me into it and believe me, it wasn't pretty."

"Dancing's not so hard. I taught myself," Merry said. "You're good with numbers. You just count to three, that's all."

Daniel quickly waved the idea off. "No, I—"

"Really. If that's all that's standing in the way of you taking Catherine to that Ball, don't worry, I'll show you," Merry encouraged. "You can practice on your own, then try it out with me later if you want."

"I really don't think—"

"Don't think," Merry said. "Just watch. And listen to the music in your head. One hand on your partner's waist, the other takes her hand, just lightly. Then, it's..." Merry closed her eyes, imagining music. She extended her arm as if being held, and three-stepped in time. "First with the left. One, two-three. Then back a little to the right, two-three. Left, two-three..."

Daniel watched Merry as she turned, a look of fascination on his face.

Suddenly self-conscious, Merry came to a stop. "So, something to consider. That is, if it suits your...situation."

Again, much to Merry's chagrin, Daniel remained enigmatic. "Yes, well—given the situation with Catherine...I may go another way."

Merry accepted it, sensing it was as far as she should go. "Okay. Let me know if you change your mind." She took her bag of discards toward the garage, quietly encouraged.

Tara was already decorating the living room mantle with holly and pine when Merry came back inside. Merry purposely didn't make anything of it, but she was quietly thrilled to see Tara taking an initiative. She watched, impressed, when Tara picked up a spool of red ribbon, pulled out a length of it, and looped it repeatedly to fashion an artful bow. If it had been a step in the right direction when Ollie had join in, Tara taking part seemed a quantum leap.

As respectfully as she could, Merry placed family photos amongst the greenery they arranged on the mantle. She picked up a photo of Amanda with the twins as grade-schoolers, dressed identically. "So, you two used to dress to match."

Tara shrugged pleasantly. "Kind of geeky, but I liked it. I guess I'm more into the whole twin thing than Hayden is." Tara picked up a particularly striking photo of her father, and drew it to Merry's attention. "Isn't this great of Dad?"

Just then, Hayden leaned in momentarily from the kitchen. "Dinner," she called.

Tara barked back, "Just a minute. Helping here."

Not wanting to get between the sisters, Merry took the photo of Daniel. "I'll get this. You go, eat. Really. It's fine."

Tara set the bow down, and then headed toward the kitchen.

Merry carefully placed the photo of Daniel at the center of the mantle. She lingered over his image, nestling it into the pine and holly boughs. It really was good of Daniel, she thought. All of his photos were. His dark hair, bright smile, and shining eyes were undeniably appealing. But mostly, she realized, it was the man himself who was starting to make her heart flutter in ways it never had before. Merry checked to make sure she was unobserved, then stroked the photo affectionately.

♥   ♥   ♥

In his pajamas, Daniel turned off the bedside lamp. Moonlight spilled through the window as Daniel stood there, deep in thought. The Charity Ball had been a reasonable idea for Catherine, he supposed. She would enjoy the opportunity to dress up and mingle with the upper echelon. Catherine was a sensation in those settings. What's more, she would be happy to write a generous check for the Children's Hospital.

Tentatively, Daniel began to practice the three-step Merry had taught him. *One, two, three...one, two, three*, he counted.

Passing by in the hall, Hayden watched her father, wryly amused. "What are you doing?"

Daniel stopped abruptly, suddenly embarrassed to realize his awkward attempt had been observed. "Nothing. Just something Merry suggested. Clearly not my skill set."

Hayden stifled a grin. "Not so much."

"Goodnight, Hayden," Daniel said as he pulled back the covers to get into bed.

"Night, Dad." Hayden padded down the hall.

Daniel sat on the bed, shaking his head at the oddity of it all.

♥　♥　♥

The wee hours of the morning found Tara hard at work, the beam of a flashlight spilling on her father's newest note to Merry. She could see that her gift idea was catching on and it encouraged her creativity.

Ollie sleepily shuffled into the study. "Did he send another one?" he wondered a bit too loudly.

"Shhh! Want him to hear us?"

Ollie nestled up to see Tara's work. "What did you do?"

Tara sat up proudly. "Turned up the flame a notch." She blew on the drying ink as Ollie read.

"You wrote *'Much Love'* this time. Oooh..."

Tara pointed out the salutation. "I also put that *'Dearest'* before Merry's name. And I'm particularly proud of this part I added at the end, here. Look. Dad had it ending with just *'everything that you are.'* But I made it *'everything that you are becoming to me.'* See? Can't even tell I added that last part."

Tara giggled conspiratorially. She stuck out a pinkie, reminding Ollie of their top-secret pact. Ollie linked his little finger with hers, grinning as he whispered. "This is gonna be good."

seven

🙰 ♥ 🙰

Morning came, and with it, anticipation over all the day could bring. As she readied herself to set off, Merry marveled. For so long, there had seemed no end to the bumpy road of her life, but now, she felt herself turning a corner. With each step, there was a growing sense that she was walking into an entirely new season.

As she locked her apartment to head out, Merry counted her blessings. Her phone, gas, electric, and credit card bills were current. There were groceries in her cupboard. Her mechanic had happily paid off her car, and then bought it as a restoration project.

Merry chuckled to herself that she didn't have to dodge Mr. Grabinski on the way to the El. Instead, she wished him a nice day, confident that her December rent check would clear. Everything in Merry's heart sang out. She was headed to work at a job she loved, working for a man who had captured her imagination.

Arriving at the Bell homestead, Merry went straight to the study. Even if she hadn't been instructed to check the Christmas drawer each morning, she still would have done so first thing. She wondered if there would be another note from Daniel and exactly what it might say.

Merry slid the desk drawer open. She was not disappointed. Again, there was no to-do list hurriedly jotted on an impersonal lined pad. Instead, there was another card in an envelope, labeled with her name.

Merry perched on the desk chair, savoring the moment. She pulled out Daniel's note, then sat back, drinking in every Tara-amended word:

Dearest Merry,

You left so quietly tonight. I didn't get a chance to say thank you. I'm so grateful for everything that you're doing—and even more for everything that you are becoming to me.

Much Love, Daniel

Fondly, Merry pressed the note to her heart. She held it out again, reading it over and over. Any doubt that the first note had left in her mind evaporated in the light of this second one.

Merry reminded herself that it was just the beginning. She knew not to leap headlong too fast. But her eyes shone at the thought of what seemed to be developing. She doubled her resolve to do everything she could to give the Bell family the best Christmas of their lives.

By the time the twins' bus dropped them off at the corner that afternoon, Merry had already added a festive wreath to the front door. She'd sealed bright red apples and affixed them to a ring of fragrant long-needle pine. Shiny jingle bells—one for each member of the family—hung at the center, sure to ring with each entrance and exit. A sheer golden bow tied it all together, sending a message that this house would indeed be celebrating the season.

Hayden trudged up as Merry began to wrap the iron rail up the steps with pine garland. Tara wasn't far behind her sister, concluding a cell phone call.

Merry greeted the girls with a smile. "Want to help deck the halls?"

Hayden shot a dull look back. "Gee. I would, but I'm, oh, so anxious to write a love sonnet for English."

"I'll help," Tara volunteered. "Already wrote my sonnet in Study Hall. I'm telling you, one look at Leo and it just fell right out of me. Borderline brilliant, and it's not even due for two weeks!"

Hayden clasped her hand over an imaginary microphone and affected her voice as if making an announcement over a loudspeaker. "Attention customers: ego overstock on aisle five."

As Hayden went inside, Tara turned back to Merry, enthused. "Okay, shhh! But I've got it! The quintessential thing for my Christmas list."

Merry's interest was immediately piqued. "Something for you?"

Tara shook her perfectly coifed head. "For Hayden, silly. Okay, this is genius! Just ask me what Hayden would want more than anything ever. Ask me!"

"What would Hayden want more than anything ever?" Merry repeated.

"Her own room!" Tara exclaimed. "We move her out, set up her own space where she can peck at all her computer dealie-bobs and mope to her heart's delight. It hit me, like, bing! Wouldn't this be absolutely perfect for her?"

Merry nodded, weighing the possibility, "Wow, and for you, too."

"Okay, this is not about me," Tara protested. "Yeah, it's a fringe, but remember, she's the one who's opted out with me ever since Mom died."

Merry secured the garland with wire. "People deal with these things in different ways.".

"It's been three years," Tara dismissed. "Kinda time to move on."

"Have you?"

Tara hesitated a bit. "Yeah, I mean—I'm not over it, over it. I still miss her, but I'm not going to spend my whole life moping, much less wreck yet another Christmas."

In some ways, Tara was right. Merry knew it, and she felt for her. "Has it been awful?"

"You have no idea," Tara confided. She put her books down and picked up a length of pine. "Dad must really like you, though. A lot."

Merry did her best not to let her growing interest in Daniel show. "What makes you think so?"

Tara was as cool as the December breeze. "Just that you have him actually enjoying this as a holiday is radical. Even if it's only to convince ourselves that this family is something approaching normal, which it so categorically isn't."

"Maybe you can change that."

"Hello?" Tara replied. "That's why the room for Hayden."

Merry pondered it, realizing that the idea might not be as self-serving or outlandish as it had first seemed. "So, where would you see her new room being? I'm new here, but I haven't found any empties."

Tara gave Merry a congenial shrug. "Oh, I don't know. Somewhere. You'll figure it out."

Merry wandered the upstairs hallway, looking into each and every room. She pushed the master suite door open and scanned the space thoughtfully. She wondered if she dared to go in, and then decided that she would. After all, how could she help the children with ideas for their father if she had no idea what he already owned?

Examining the top of Daniel's dresser, Merry smiled, noticing a collection of tiny, wind-up toys. There were more robots, some animals, and racecars. Merry picked up a bottle of Daniel's cologne and took in the musky aroma with recognition. She had noticed that scent from the first time she'd bumped into him and spilled coffee all over his suit.

Merry glanced around. *There it is*, she thought. There was that suit, hanging in a dry cleaning bag on the hook outside his closet door. Daniel had been so good about that, she recalled. He'd never so much as mentioned it again. What a man did when you spilled something on him said a lot to Merry. She didn't do it often, but she'd spilled enough on Arthur's customers to know it could bring out the worst or the best.

Ollie peered into his father's room. "Whatcha doing?"

Merry startled. "Ah! Ollie!" She quickly recapped the cologne and put it back in place on the dresser. "Just, uh, looking for something," she improvised.

Ollie wandered in. "Can I help?"

"Well, um...that depends."

Ollie eyed Merry suspiciously. "On what?"

Merry stepped to the door and mysteriously cased the hallway. "Can you be trusted with highly classified intel? Information that, if divulged, could put major sticks in your stocking?"

Moments later, Ollie tiptoed down the hall. He peeked into the twins' room like a secret agent. A finger to the side of his nose, Ollie slyly signaled Merry that the coast was clear.

Ollie slinked past. Merry followed. Ollie ran and flattened himself against the doorjamb at the end of the hall. Playing along, Merry pressed herself against the wall beside him. Ollie nodded the *all clear* signal.

"Cover me," Merry whispered.

Ollie raised an imaginary pistol, checking down the hallway as Merry slipped by him, turned the doorknob and cracked it open.

When Merry peered in, she found herself at the bottom of a steep attic staircase. Ollie tipped his head in below her, a landslide grin unfurling at the prospects.

As soon as she got to the top of the stairs, Merry pulled out her phone.

"Who are you calling?" Ollie asked.

"I'm texting Tara. Your dad gave me her number." Merry keyed in a message as she spoke. *"Ix-nay on ayden-Hay. Upstairs."* Merry sent the text, and then stepped into the cluttered attic room. Dormer windows sent light streams through dust particles, falling on a host of stored items. There was old furniture, the kids' former cribs, and toys they'd grown past. There were boxes, trunks, and suitcases from long ago family vacations.

"You come up here much?" Merry asked.

Ollie shook his head. "Dad says I can't without a grown-up. I think 'cause of mom's stuff. But I still like it."

Merry examined the markings on a stack of boxes marked *Christmas*. "Well, lookee here."

Ollie threw back a tarp, launching a cloud of dust just as Tara reached the landing. Tara dodged, waving the dust off vigorously. "Hey, watch it. This is dry clean only."

Merry gestured toward the attic room. "Tara...I think we've found your present."

"Like I want a bunch of dusty old relics," Tara groused.

Ollie rolled his eyes. "For Hayden, Dopey. The room?"

Tara shot a betrayed look at Merry. "You told him?!"

"Well, yeah," Merry defended, "And if you're nice to him, he might help you fix it up for her."

"And keep all our other secrets," Ollie added, with a broad wink at Tara.

Tara back-peddled, confused. "Wait a minute. I'm supposed to fix this whole mess up? You misunderstand. I'm more of an idea person."

"But, you also execute," Merry noted. "Like your love sonnet and all your outfits. Who puts things together better than you?"

Tara seemed to warm to the idea. "I do have a knack," she observed. "And Hayden is definitely challenged in the style department."

Merry threw an arm around Tara, leading her into the room. "So, we'll get the extra stuff out, open up some space for you to do your wonders, and divert Hayden's attention while you're up here."

"No need," Tara sighed dejectedly. "She won't even miss me."

When Merry dropped by the study to get her coat that evening, she found Daniel at his desk, taking care of the family bills. She popped her head in cheerily. "Knock, knock."

Daniel motioned Merry in, a welcoming expression on his face. "So, Tara brought me into the loop about the attic."

"And you're okay with it?"

Daniel nodded approvingly. "I like it that you think outside the ordinary Christmas box."

Merry ventured into the room. "Speaking of 'out there' gift ideas—for your mom, along those lines... What about an invitation to live here?"

Daniel sat back. "Where here? It's not like I have any more attics."

Merry moved closer. "Well, she said you don't use this office much. And there's plenty of space in the master suite for your desk."

Daniel smiled pleasantly. "So, you've been exploring, haven't you?"

Merry blushed. "You said to listen for hints, which have pretty much been flying like snowballs."

"She said she wants to move in here?"

"Not in so many words," Merry explained. "But...sometimes you can tell what's inside a package without opening it."

Daniel studied Merry for a moment. "Yes, you seem to have a talent for that. But I was thinking she might like a nice sweater, maybe a coat. Or a sweater coat. That would be good."

Though everything inside Merry screamed that his idea wasn't the best, she was careful not to overstep. "Good. I'll pick something out. But, I'm sure she'd love it if we could work the room out, too. That is, only if you want that."

Daniel put his checkbook aside, weighing the notion fondly. "There you go," he said. "Once again, you're as wily as Amanda. When we bought this house, I'll admit I deliberately put this desk here, staked out the territory so that—"

"—So she wouldn't feel staked out," Merry finished.

The look on Daniel's face said it all. Merry knew immediately that she had dug down to the truth, a truth Daniel hid, even from himself.

"I adore my mother," he confided. "The kids love her to pieces. But down the block is close enough, all things considered."

Merry drifted by Daniel's desk. "Funny thing is, if I had a mom as great as yours, I don't think I could keep her close enough."

Daniel shook his head, resisting. "But, given where I'm heading with things, the truth is..."

Daniel motioned Merry closer. When she stepped just to the side of his desk, he lowered his voice to a confidential tone. "If and when another woman moves into this house," Daniel said, "I've been looking for the kind of woman that..." Again, he paused. "The truth is, I was hoping that she'd be my wife."

No more words passed between them that night. Daniel simply punctuated his point with a smile that said he had a specific woman in mind.

Though she thought she'd burst with joy, Merry held her composure, wanting to allow Daniel to take things at his own pace. In the past, she'd made the mistake of gulping too soon. This time, she resolved, she would sip and savor what was developing between them, every delicious step of the way.

Merry nodded to Daniel that she understood, an effervescent sparkle in her eyes. With a simple wave goodbye, she slipped out for the evening, wondering if there'd be a way in the world that she'd sleep a single wink that night.

eight
❧ ♥ ❧

Merry navigated the Bell's upstairs hallway, her arms overloaded with Christmas boxes from the attic. Indeed, it was a precarious pile, but she'd picked it up with a special purpose. As she passed the twins' bedroom, Merry peered in at Hayden who sat, staring blankly at her computer screen. "Think you could give me a hand?"

Hayden pushed her laptop away in frustration. "I guess," she sighed, "now that I've made so much progress on my sonnet."

Outwardly, Merry made nothing of it as Hayden came to her aid, but inside, Merry celebrated. Her idea had worked. It was only a foot in the door with Hayden, but Merry knew it was a start.

Downstairs, Merry sorted through the tiny houses and storefronts of a miniature village as Hayden pulled out pieces of a model train set. Merry didn't mention it, but she presumed that every piece of that railway represented a memory, a connection to Christmases long ago. All of those memories had been good, she supposed, all except the very last one.

"Looks like I'm not the only one that's been living under the tracks," Merry quipped.

"Yeah, this is all Dad's," Hayden replied. "Mom started it for him. First the engine, couple of cars. Never did get a caboose."

Merry nodded softly, steeling herself to take the plunge. "Is it okay if I ask you something?"

Hayden grimaced wryly. "Just don't go all Barbara Walters on me."

Merry snapped two track pieces together. "What was your mom like?"

Hayden shrugged. The subtlest sort of smiles crossed her face. "She was...kind of corny but cool, about Christmas and Valentines and birthdays and pretty much any other excuse to do her whole uber-mom thing. Freakish you should ask about her because it's sort of taboo here."

"You know, you're really pretty when you smile like that," Merry observed.

"I'm not smiling," Hayden replied.

"Not now. But you were."

Hayden quickly dropped back to a smirk. "Promise not to hold it against me."

Merry nodded. "Promise. But I think the moratorium on enjoying Christmas ran out a while ago. You could always ease your way back into it. Don't want to crack anything. Start with a warm-fuzzy, barely there," Merry playfully demonstrated as she spoke. "Then, a sort of botoxed upper lip smile."

Hayden bit her lip, but Merry still spotted it.

"Busted!" Merry teased. "You're such a little cheater!"

Losing the battle, Hayden clamped her lips with her fingers.

Merry pointed at Hayden with glee. "Flag on the play! No lip biting or finger clamping!"

Despite Hayden's concerted efforts to prevent it, a grin popped out.

"Ring-a-ling! Somebody get a camera!" Merry exuded.

"Cut it out!" Hayden protested. "You're as bad as mom!"

Merry tipped her head a little. "Well, thanks, Hayden. That was a very nice thing to say."

"Yeah, well you... She..." Tears sprang to Hayden's eyes.

Immediately, Merry's heart went out to her. She put a hand on her arm. "Oh, Hayden. I'm sorry."

Hayden quickly shook Merry's hand off. "Forget it, all right?"

"You know it's okay to—"

"No, it's not okay," Hayden broke in, her emotions clearly rising. "I hate this. All of it! All it does is remind me what I can't ever have again. You know what I want for Christmas? I want my mom back. Can you get me that?"

Merry held Hayden's demanding gaze. "Sweetie, I wish I could."

Hayden jerked away. "And don't call me that!" she cried. "That's what she called me. Nobody calls me that."

"Maybe they should," Merry persisted. "Maybe she'd want them to. Like she'd want to know you found a way, well, not to forget her, but to enjoy the life she gave you."

Hayden wiped her face. It was a long while before she finally spoke. "I don't know how to do that."

Tears brimmed in Merry's eyes as she searched Hayden's. "I just know, every day you had with your mom—every time you get another day with your dad, your sister, Ollie, your grandmom—it's a incredible gift. I don't know much, Hayden. But I know that."

Hayden sat silently, irony playing on her face. "Funny that you'd mention gifts. I know exactly what to give Tara for Christmas. It's just really hard to give it. I don't know if I can."

Merry nodded thoughtfully. "You know, I always thought that the gifts that are hardest to give, well...they can be the best gifts of all."

Christmas music wafted from an old-fashioned turntable, filling the Bell's garage. Familiar tunes from a by-gone era scratched out, sung by crooners of long ago holidays, the kind that set a person swaying, no matter the task they accompanied.

Ollie helped Merry stow attic overflow in the unoccupied half of the garage. Ollie was a good helper, Merry observed. He'd taken to her from the start, something she dearly appreciated. He needed a mother as much as Hayden did, she realized. He just showed it in different ways.

Ollie's face lit up as the garage door began to open and Daniel's headlights shone into the garage. "Daddy's home!" Ollie exuded. Ollie ran to greet his dad as the car idled outside.

Merry hustled to move a few items aside. "Just a sec. I'll get this out of your way. Sorry. I had thought you'd park out front."

Daniel pulled into his parking space in the garage. "Well, the forecast says we might get some snow, so... What's all this?" he wondered, turning his car off.

Merry glanced around. "Attic overflow."

"Don't tell Hayden," Ollie added urgently.

"Right," Daniel agreed. "Hey, Buddy, why don't you go wash up for dinner. I'll get this."

Obediently, Ollie ran toward the townhouse. Daniel began to help Merry stow things they haven't used in years—a cradle, the twins' double stroller, Ollie's tricycle.

"That was my dad's old turntable over there," Daniel recalled. "Obsolete now, I guess. Amazing that it still works. Looks like we're way overdue for a purge."

Merry looked around, imagining the long ago time when these things had been in regular use. "Everything here has a place in your family story, I'm sure."

Daniel nodded nostalgically. "Really does. Christmas used to be a big day around here."

"I can tell," Merry said. "It can be again, you know."

Daniel hoisted a box. "Sure hope so."

Merry helped Daniel to slide the container in place. "Yeah. Me, too," she replied. Suddenly, an idea struck. "You know what?" she said. "Close your eyes. Go on, close them."

Going along with it, Daniel closed his eyes. Merry quickly plugged in an electrical cord, then lightly took Daniel by the hand and led him out of the garage. She loved the way he trusted her as she guided him all the way into the back yard, his eyes still shut tight. Classic Christmas music from the open garage wafted across the night air.

"Not yet. No peeking," Merry reminded.

As they passed the kitchen window, Merry noticed Ollie and Tara, watching from inside. Merry put a finger to her lips, signaling them about the secret she was preparing to unfold. Tara broke into a victorious grin. Ollie playfully poked her.

Reaching the patio, Merry led Daniel to a stopping place.

"Now?" Daniel asked.

Merry released his hand. "Now."

Daniel opened his eyes. The yard was aglow with twinkle lights. Strings of lights hung on fence rails, shrubs and trees, shimmering all around them. Daniel took it all in, then looked back at Merry, completely amazed.

Merry smiled softly. "Starting to feel like Christmas, now, isn't it?"

Daniel nodded. "It is."

"Sure you don't want to take me up on that dancing lesson?" Merry offered.

Daniel paused. "I confess...I'm still back and forth about what to do for Catherine. I'm not sure if the Ball is really the right thing."

Merry weighed her options. It wasn't she wanted Daniel to opt to take Catherine to the Charity Ball, but something in her had to know for sure. "You know, if you got more comfy with the dancing part, you could set that aside," Merry suggested. "Might help you to see the rest of the decision more clearly."

Merry offered her right hand to Daniel. Warily, he took it. "Then you pull your partner close, so you can feel how she's moving," Merry instructed.

As Daniel drew Merry next to him, the warmth of his nearness went all through her.

"I'm afraid you'll need to lead," he confessed.

"That's okay," Merry answered. "Just take it when you're ready. I'll sense it."

Thousands of lights illuminated as Merry and Daniel began to waltz around the patio. They were tentative at first, but before long they had lost themselves in the moment.

♥   ♥   ♥

Hours after Merry had left for the diner, Daniel sat at his desk, half paying the bills and half deep in thought. The decision about what to get Catherine for Christmas weighed heavily on his mind. She was a woman who already had everything, he thought, everything that money could buy.

In the five months since he'd met Catherine, she hadn't once asked him for anything beyond the pleasure of his company. There'd been no occasion for gifts yet, no birthdays to pass, nor any material need. What he'd found they had in common was a deeper longing, a desire for companionship.

It wasn't that attraction hadn't played a role, but there was a genuine quality beneath Catherine's refined beauty, something of substance that had captured his attention. Perhaps it had been their intersecting career paths that had drawn them together; perhaps it was her sparkling intellect. But whatever it was, it had made him believe he could love again. For years, he had thought of no other woman than the wife he'd lost. Yet, from the moment Catherine had come into his life, something had been reawakened.

The ringing phone brought Daniel out of his reverie. He could see from his Caller ID that it was

Catherine. Daniel picked up. "I was just thinking of you."

"Really?" Catherine replied. "Because I was just talking about you. With Daddy. I'm afraid the cat's out of the bag."

"And which cat would that be?"

Catherine paused coyly. "Let's just say, he approves. Highly."

Daniel listened with interest. "Oh?"

"He said...so many things," Catherine went on. "How he trusts you, that you're a man of your word—and what else—ah, yes, that a man of your particular 'intentions' toward me would be most welcome to, let's say, advance within the Strong family. Banking and otherwise."

Though, as usual, the meaning of Catherine's words wasn't conclusive on the surface, her subtext rang through loud and clear to Daniel. Indeed, he was a man of his word. He had expressed his sincere intentions to Catherine. She had voiced his stated interest to her father, his boss, and the idea had met with the soon-retiring bank president's resounding endorsement.

Though they chatted on about the minutia of the day, Daniel rocked back in his chair, reflecting on the big picture of their lives. Every romance comes to a crossroads, he realized, a pivotal point of decision. As he listened to the happiness in Catherine's voice, he knew that—one way or another—the time had come.

♥   ♥   ♥

At the Downtown Diner, Merry counted tips as Kiki closed out the register. It had been a good night.

"And how long did this dancing lesson go on?" Kiki inquired.

"Two, three minutes," Merry smiled. "Even though it still doesn't seem like he wants to take Catherine to that Ball. Afterward, he said he might go another way with her gift."

Kiki closed the cash drawer. "So, next, float something more businessy for her. See it he latches onto that. Any more love notes yet?"

"Just the one I'm working on," Merry glowed. "I'll leave it in the drawer tomorrow night."

Just then, Merry's cell phone rang. To her delight, a look at the screen confirmed that it was Daniel. Purposefully, she walked away from Arthur's earshot to answer. "Hey, Daniel...all right...Uh-huh...Yeah. I got it...Sure. See you there." With that, Merry hung up. She returned wordlessly and started to wipe the counter, covering her excitement as much as she could.

"Oh, no," Kiki insisted. "No, no. What did he say?"

Merry played it down. "No biggie."

Kiki put on her sassy-pants voice. "Then why your eyes popping half out your head?"

Merry glanced to the kitchen to see if Arthur was listening. He was. Caught, Arthur resumed cleaning the grill.

Under her breath, Merry whispered to Kiki. "He just... The things he says... This could be going somewhere."

Kiki reared back, thrilled. "You have got it bad."

"I'm supposed to meet him downtown at noon tomorrow," Merry enthused. "He wants to take me shopping."

Kiki mouth dropped open. "He. Mr. Ritzy Bank man, taking you shopping? That's what he's paying you to do!"

Merry leaned in. "Which is why I think it has nothing to do with the job and everything to do with what he said is happening between us."

"Where's he taking you?" Kiki probed.

"I dunno," Merry replied. "He just said it'd be our secret till Christmas."

Long after her normal bedtime, Merry sat, curled up on her bed, writing a draft of a note. Rudy purred lazily at her side.

"Okay, how does this sound, Rudy?" Merry held the paper up and read aloud: *"Dearest Daniel..."* She stopped, hesitant about her choice. "Should I say dearest? He did. Maybe I... Ah, I know..." Merry scribbled in a change, then resumed the recitation:

My dear Daniel,

I can hardly even write those words or wrap my head around the idea that this could possibly be. But it is, and you are, all part of the wonder that is this Christmas. You've been so brave to take the lead, to say so much more than I've been able to, but now I want you to see my answer plainly—right here, in my hand. My heart is yours, Daniel.

Merry stroked Rudy's back. "That's it, boy, isn't it?" Her eyes shining with hope, she reached for a small shopping bag and pulled out a tiny, wind-up kangaroo. "Look what I found. It's a hopper. Like me," she explained to Rudy. "I'm saving it for his Christmas." Merry set the toy aside and gazed contentedly at her note to Daniel. "This, he'll get tomorrow."

nine

❧ ♥ ❧

Excited at the prospect of shopping with Daniel, Merry had arrived early. As she sat waiting on a bench, she looked around at the uptown retail district. There were ritzy boutiques, high-end eateries, and posh gift shops that the well-to-do frequented. It was so far out of Merry's economic stratum that she'd never even window-shopped there before. She'd always been far more of a discount store type, but this was the place where Daniel had invited her to meet him, just a few blocks from Strong Bank & Trust.

Mid-day traffic rumbled by as Merry read over her card to Daniel, confirming to herself that she'd said everything she wanted so much to say to him.

She reminded herself that, since he had sent her two notes, the ball was in her court to reply.

Suddenly, Daniel rounded the corner on foot. Merry quickly stowed her note for later, gathered her bags, and rose to greet him.

"There you are," Daniel called out. "Sorry I'm a little late, but—"

"No, it's fine," Merry insisted, showing him one of her parcels. "I just picked up a few doodads at the market along the way."

Daniel beamed at Merry. It seemed to her that he was every bit as energized about the excursion as she was.

"So, here we are," he acknowledged.

Merry nodded. "Yes. Here we are."

"You'll have to forgive me if I'm a bit nervous about this," Daniel started. "I guess we haven't known each other that long. I mean, it feels like we practically just met, but we're not kids anymore and... Well, sometimes you just have to go for it."

Merry took Daniel's words to heart. It was true that they hadn't known each other very long, but something undeniable was growing between them. She leaned toward him reassuringly. "You do have to go for it sometimes, and—don't you think surprises, coming right out of the blue—isn't that the best part of Christmas?"

"It is," Daniel agreed. "But in this case, at least everyone else will be surprised and...I just thought it would be better if you were with me. If you could tell me what you like...that would really help take the worries out of choosing." Daniel gestured toward the corner.

As Merry turned, he briefly guided her with a genteel hand on her back. It had just been a momentary brush, but the memory of his touch lingered. Even through her woolen coat, it had warmed her through and through.

As Daniel's destination became clear, Merry's heart skipped a beat. This was to be no casual gift, she realized. Daniel planned to shop with her for jewelry.

Everything inside the opulent jewelry store glimmered. Precious gemstones set in gold and platinum rested on velvet inside gleaming glass cases. Fine silver services were polished to perfection. Merry looked around, overwhelmed as Daniel approached a dark-suited salesperson. Clearly, only the wealthy frequented this place.

"That one. There—first from the left on the second row," Daniel directed.

The salesperson bowed his head respectfully as he unlocked the case. "Excellent, Sir. Just a moment."

Daniel motioned Merry over as the salesperson pulled out an exquisite ring and handed it to Daniel. A princess cut diamond flanked by radiant sapphires shone in an elegant platinum setting. "I saw this yesterday afternoon," Daniel said, "And I just had to be sure."

Merry watched, stunned as Daniel held the ring up toward the plate glass window. Prisms of light danced on the many facets of the diamond. Merry swallowed hard. Had it been a bracelet or earrings, she might have reacted differently, but clearly, this was an engagement ring.

Despite everything that seemed to have been happening between them, and as much as Merry wished she could believe otherwise, something told her that she must have completely misunderstood. It was far too much, and far too soon. Merry's heart sank as she realized the crushing truth:

This gift was for Catherine.

With everything in her, Merry fought the tears that threatened. The last thing she wanted Daniel to see was how distraught she was, or how mortified she felt at having read more into his notes than he seemed to have intended.

"Well... What do you think? Will she like it?" Daniel asked. He handed the ring to Merry for a closer look.

Merry gazed at the ring, doing her best to form a response, to find some honest way to be happy for him. She couldn't say how broken-hearted she was. She couldn't speak to his now-obvious interest in Catherine. She could only focus her answer on the ring itself. "Daniel, it's...it's completely stunning. She'll love it," Merry said. "It's the most beautiful ring I've ever seen."

"Would you mind trying it on for her?" Daniel inquired.

Reflexively, Merry handed the ring back to Daniel. "No... No, I couldn't. "

"Sure. That's why I called you," Daniel protested. "I'm dying to see how it would look."

Before she could stop him, Daniel took her left hand in his. He slid the ring onto Merry's finger. It was almost more than she could bear. Merry gazed at the ring on her hand, both dazzled and devastated. "We'll probably have to get it sized," she noted.

"It fits you amazingly," Daniel observed. "I wonder how close you are to Catherine's size."

Through her pain, Merry willed a bittersweet smile. "I don't know," she said. "My hand versus Catherine's—it probably doesn't compare."

♥ ♥ ♥

Merry approached Joan's pottery shop on foot, barely holding it together. She had no idea who else to turn to at that moment, no one who would understand like Daniel's mother.

As she opened the door, she saw Joan, gliding through a class of senior women as they beat the air bubbles out of balls of clay, slamming them against a canvas-covered table. Merry's eyes brimmed at just the sight of Joan. "Could I come in?"

Joan turned from her pottery students. "Sure, we were...." Joan immediately read the distress on Merry's face. "Merry, what's wrong?"

The quiver on Merry's lips quickly gave way to open sobs. Joan rushed to her side. "Baby, what is it?"

"He's buying the china!" Merry blurted, tears coursing down her cheeks.

Joan embraced Merry, patting her back as she wept. The women in Joan's class couldn't help but notice, so Joan attempted an explanation.

"She's a purist."

With that, Joan guided Merry out back. She grabbed a wad of tissue along the way and handed it to Merry. "There you go."

Merry wiped her face. She blew her reddened nose. "Thanks for letting me come here. I didn't know where else to—"

"You can come here anytime," Joan assured.

"No matter what dishes he buys?"

"No matter what," Joan replied. "Always. You hear me?"

Merry stepped away, out of the class's earshot. "I really thought we were connecting, but I...I must have read him all wrong," she rued. "Guess I just got caught up in this ridiculous hope that he could actually love me, that I could somehow be part of this family."

Joan took Merry's face in her hands and looked her square in the eyes. "You *are* part of this family," she insisted. "Just a couple of weeks and... Look at this." Joan showed Merry a shelf of freshly thrown plates, drying on a nearby rack.

Merry looked on, amazed. "You made those?"

"That's right. I made them because of you," Joan replied. "And there's a piece of you in every one they'll eat off, every single Christmas from now on. China or no china, Merry, you've already put your fingerprints all over us."

The faintest kind of hope broke through Merry's tears. "I have?"

Joan nodded. "We've needed you, Merry. We still need you. Whether my blind-as-a-bat son can see it or not."

♥   ♥   ♥

Later that afternoon, Tara and Ollie led a blindfolded Merry up the attic stairs.

"Are you taking me where I think you're taking me?" Merry inquired.

Ollie replied in his deepest belly-shaking voice. "Ho, ho, ho! Might be someplace secret!"

Tara whipped around to her brother. "Shhh! Hayden will hear."

Feeling her way toward the landing at the top, Merry tripped, and then righted herself.

Ceremoniously, Tara reached to untie Merry's blindfold. "And now, the moment we've all been waiting for," Tara announced with a signal to Ollie. "Cue the silent drum roll."

Ollie beat his leg like an imaginary drum, then hit an air cymbal. "Ching!"

Tara adopted a dramatic air, "Presenting..." Then she ripped off Merry's blindfold and flicked on the lights.

Merry scanned the completely redecorated attic, agape. Tara had done absolute wonders. "It's like...a Christmas miracle!" Merry exclaimed.

Tara shrugged with wry confidence. "Not exactly my taste, but I think the cave-dweller will like it."

That evening, the Bells served up dinner off the stove as Merry gathered her things to head to the diner for a couple of hours work.

Joan ladled a hearty chili into the family's waiting bowls. "You sure you can't stay, Merry?"

"Gramma made brownies for dessert," Ollie enthused.

"Come on, Merry. Stay," Tara coaxed. "Why not?"

Daniel picked up an extra bowl and offered it to Merry. "Please. There's plenty."

Merry put up a polite hand of refusal. Staying for dinner would be too hard for her on this particular night. "Thanks, but Friday nights are busy at the diner and I promised Arthur—"

"Ooh, Arthur," Hayden teased. "Who is this Arthur?"

Merry shook her head, "Oh, no. No, no. He's..."

Merry could feel Daniel watching as she exchanged an awkward glance with Joan. Tara gave Ollie an "*I dunno*" shrug.

Daniel smiled inquisitively, "Merry, have you been keeping something from us? Mom, what do you know?"

Feigning sincerity, Hayden pretended to swoon. "Is he super-duper dreamy?"

"No, really," Merry defended. "He's just my other boss."

"Oooh...workplace romance," Hayden toyed. "Scandalous!"

"Guys!" Merry blurted. "I'm not interested in Arthur."

A hopeful look crossed Ollie's face. "So, who are you interested in?"

Suddenly, the teasing stopped as everyone waited for an answer to Ollie's question. Merry shot a panicky look at Joan as Tara smacked Ollie upside the head.

Joan grabbed some tongs, "Ollie, dear, don't you want some salad?"

Grateful for the reprieve, Merry backed toward the door. "You know what? I'm just going to go. But I will see you all bright and early, dressed and ready for a little hunting expedition. You, too, Daniel. Remember, this is a whole family deal."

"Wouldn't miss it," Daniel replied. "I invited Catherine, too. I hope that's okay."

Merry polled the family's faces. Hayden rolled her eyes. Tara grimaced. Ollie gagged. Even Joan's expression was lackluster. With everything she had, Merry willed herself to muster support. "As they say, the more the merrier."

Daniel turned to his kids. "I know you're all just getting to know Catherine, but give it a little time," he assured. "She'll fit right in."

When it had rained overnight, Merry had been a little concerned about the outing she'd planned, but the showers had given way to the brightest of blue skies by Saturday morning. How long it had been since the family had gone anywhere together, Merry didn't know, but from the sounds of things, it seemed as if it'd been a very long while. At any rate, there was no shortage of animated chatter in the Range Rover as Daniel drove them out of town to their destination: a large hillside Christmas tree farm.

As soon as Daniel parked, the Bell clan burst out of the auto and onto the softened sandy road by the farm's gate. Old sneakers and hiking shoes hit the ground running. As Merry and the family set out, Daniel circled the car and opened the passenger door for Catherine. He offered her his hand as she stepped out onto the road, shod in high-heeled calfskin boots.

Squish!

"Oh, my," Catherine reacted as her designer footprint sunk into the moist roadbed.

"Here. Take my arm," Daniel offered.

Joan grabbed the photo op with her camera. "Lovely boots, dear. You'll have to tell me where you got them."

As they started down the road, Merry and Joan shared a knowing glance as Catherine attempted to keep up with the kids, who were already heading toward the hillside tree farm. Daniel willingly extended his arm for Catherine, but with each step, her slender heels sunk deep into the soft dirt.

Catherine turned penitently to Daniel. "I don't know what I was thinking."

Daniel offered his arm. "That's quite all right. Here. I'll help you."

Galloping ahead, Ollie called back to the family. "Come on! Hurry!"

"Plenty of trees here, Ollie," Daniel called.

"Yeah, but we have to get the best one," Ollie reminded.

Feeling awful for Catherine, Merry sidled up to her. "You can wear my boots if you want."

Catherine took a gander at Merry's thrift store combat boots. "Oh, no. I couldn't," she demured.

"My socks are plenty thick," Merry explained. "I can just wear them and throw them in the wash later."

Catherine waved Merry off. "No, no. You go. Please." Catherine turned to Daniel, clearly embarrassed. "I'm so sorry, Daniel. Go on. Find something wonderful. I'll wait here."

Minus Catherine, the Bells happily tromped up the tree-covered hillside. Merry conducted them in song as they hiked, her voice ringing across the hillside:

> *O, Christmas tree*
> *O, Christmas tree*
> *How lovely are thy branches*
> *Ba-da-dee-da-dee-da-dee-dah*
> *I do not know the other words*

"Everybody!" Merry called out, returning to the familiar lyrics of the chorus. All the Bells joined in singing. Even Hayden, a little:

> *O, Christmas tree*
> *O, Christmas tree*
> *How lovely are thy branches*

It was a wonderland of balsam and fir, but Ollie's eyes lit up, seeing a towering scotch pine. "Dad, look! Look! That's it!"

Daniel shielded his eyes from the sun as he surveyed the sky-scraping selection. "Impressive, but we'd have to vault the ceiling for that one."

Suddenly, Tara stopped in her tracks. "Oh, seriously. Everybody freeze!" Tara ordered. "There it is. That's our tree. It's just like Mom used to get us." Tara pointed joyfully to a lovely balsam fir, fanning her brimming eyes. The family gazed at the tree with fond recognition. Tara was right. In the best sort of way, it brought Amanda's memory into the season.

Moments later, Merry set up a family photo around the Bell's chosen tree. "Closer, everybody. You, too, Hayden."

"I'm leaving space for you," Hayden explained.

"That's okay. I'll just take the picture," Merry replied.

Quickly, Joan called out. "Set the timer and run over."

Daniel motioned Merry over enthusiastically. "Yeah. You should be in this, too."

Shyly grateful to be included, Merry set the timer. She dashed over as the family counted down.

"Ten, nine, eight, seven, six, five, four, three, two..."

Merry slid into place, just in the nick of time. Though the air was brisk, something in her melted inside as Daniel put a hand on her shoulder and the camera snapped the shot.

Back at the foot of the hill, Merry stood with Daniel as he settled up for their purchase. As soon as Merry saw the tree farmer reach for a sprig of mistletoe, she saw it coming. She tried to wave the farmer off, but before she could, he playfully dangled it over them. "Should I throw in a little mistletoe for you and the missus?" he teased.

Merry took an awkward step away.

Daniel quickly sputtered, "Oh, she's not...we're not—"

"Just the tree is fine, thanks," Merry replied before wandering aside.

The tree farmer laughed heartily at his gaffe. "She's a honey, all right. The tree, that is. I'll have her dug, bagged up, and delivered by sundown tomorrow."

Ollie pulled at Merry's coat. "Aren't we going to chop it down?"

Merry leaned down to Ollie. "These trees stay alive. We'll plant it in the yard after, to grow, maybe tall as that other one you spotted."

As they all headed toward the car, Daniel turned to Merry. "This is so much better than a cut tree lot. How'd you find this place?"

Merry exchanged a grin with her collaborator. "Actually, Hayden found it for me. On the Net. Her gift to the family."

Pleased, Daniel took a gander at his melancholy baby. "Well, how about that. Getting into the swing of things after all, aren't you?"

Hayden shuffled along, chagrined. "Maybe a little."

Merry poked Hayden playfully. "There it is, again. Blinding, that smile!"

Hayden broke into a snarky grin as Ollie bounded ahead with glee. "Ho, ho, ho! Merrrrrrry Christmas!" he shouted.

As they headed down the dirt road to the car, Joan and Merry brought up the rear. Joan threw an affectionate arm around Merry's shoulders. "You really are quite something," Joan assured.

Merry walked arm-in-arm with Joan, all the way to the car. Joan drew Merry especially close as Daniel greeted Catherine. "You okay?" she whispered.

Merry nodded, then climbed into the back seat. She realized that, despite her disappointment with Daniel, something very meaningful had taken root with Joan. Never in all of her life had Merry felt so cared for by an older woman. Joan was right. There was something very special between them, a kinship that transcended the seasonal bounds of temporary jobs or even blood relations. *Maybe this is what it feels like to be adopted,* Merry thought. *Maybe this is what it's like to have a mother.*

ten

What exactly it was about classic carols that made it feel all the more like Christmas, Merry didn't know. But as soon as she brought the turntable in from the garage and began to play their old holiday albums, something palpable changed in the Bell household. The sound of those songs filled the living room and the Spirit of the season came with them.

It might have been three years since they'd decorated a Christmas tree together, but as soon as their chosen fir was set in place, each family member found a way to contribute to the festivities. Tara helped her Dad wire the tree with vintage bubble lights. Joan tucked a skirt her mother had quilted around the tree's base. Merry and Ollie hung ornaments, blending family favorites from years past with their new broken china creations. Hayden connected the train cars and set them up to circle around the perimeter. Catherine settled into a soft chair, stringing cranberries together with popcorn.

Once the lights were in place, Daniel pulled out the old star they'd always put at the top of the tree. "So, who's going to do the honors?" he asked.

Ollie raised his hand immediately. "I will! I will!"

"You should, Daniel," Merry suggested.

"No, no," Daniel insisted. "Their mom always had us settle this by acclaim." With that, Daniel raised the star over his son's head. "Everyone for Ollie."

Ollie egged on enthusiastic clapping. Merry put two fingers in her mouth and added a sharp whistle. Next, Daniel moved the star over his mom, then Tara and Hayden. One by one, all received supportive hoots and hollers. Even Catherine got a modicum of polite applause.

Daniel stopped and scanned the group. "Now, let's see. Who haven't we tried?"

"Merry! Try Merry!" Ollie exclaimed.

Merry shyly deferred. "No, really."

Suddenly, Tara began to chant Merry's name. Ollie, Joan and Hayden joined in. "Mer-ry! Mer-ry! Mer-ry! Mer-ry!"

"The tribe has spoken," Daniel joked, and with a polite bow, he handed the star to Merry.

Merry shot a concerned glance at Catherine. "Don't you want to do this?"

Catherine masked her feelings well. "No, no. Go ahead. I have my hands full here."

Joan took a seat by Catherine. "Here, let me help you with that," she offered.

Daniel steadied the ladder beside the tree as Merry climbed. When she reached the next to the last step, Merry saw that the treetop was still out of reach. "Remind me to ask for stilts next year," she said.

"Hey, you could borrow Catherine's boots," Hayden teased, enjoying the snickers it drew from her siblings.

"Okay, okay. I know I deserved that," smiled Catherine.

Daniel looked up at Merry. "We'll get you there," he promised, turning to his daughter. "Hayden, hold this, will you?"

Hayden secured the ladder. Daniel extended his hand to Merry, steadying her to mount the top step. "Here you go," he offered.

"Here I go," Merry echoed, climbing to the tiptop. "Oh, boy..." Merry stretched to set the star. It was still a bit precarious.

"Wait a sec," Daniel instructed. "I got you."

Daniel took hold of Merry's waist to steady her, wreaking jolly havoc on her heart. Supported by Daniel, Merry leaned to place the star. She slid it into place, provoking a round of jubilant cheers.

But... As Merry turned, beaming, she started to wobble.

"Wuh-oh!" Hayden blurted, grabbing for the ladder too late.

Merry swung her arms to right herself, but it was to no avail.

"Timber!" Ollie shouted. As if in slow motion, the Bells tried to prevent the inevitable. Catherine jumped out of the fray. Daniel dove as Merry tumbled headlong from the ladder, the light cord pulling the tree down. Daniel caught Merry as she fell, and the whole family dominoed to the floor, convulsing with laughter.

The next thing Merry knew, she was flat on the carpet, face to face with Daniel, entwined in his arms, the tree on top of them. Merry couldn't help the sparks that flew inside her.

Daniel held Merry's gaze while Joan helped the kids pull the fallen tree off of them. "You okay?"

"Yeah, I'm fine," Merry answered. "I'm good."

In seconds, the tree was righted. Merry sat up and Daniel rose to help the kids reset the tree. It had only been a moment, but Merry had seen the look on Catherine's face.

Catherine had been gracious. She'd resumed stringing popcorn with cranberries without a word. Still, Merry knew that the incident had far from escaped her notice.

♥ ♥ ♥

Catherine parked her Mercedes outside Arthur's Downtown Diner. Warily, she eyed the sketchy neighborhood. Sparse streetlights cast an amber glow over a part of town Catherine never visited at night, not unless absolutely necessary. She sat for a moment, hoping against hope that the homeless man out front would go away.

He didn't.

As scary as it was to contemplate leaving the safety of her car, it was all the more frightening for Catherine to let her mission go unaccomplished, so she opened the door and got out. Immediately, the homeless man took a step in her direction and held up his "Will Work For Food" sign. Spooked by him, she quickly set her alarm.

"Name's Skeeter, Ma'am. Sure is a pretty car," the homeless man noted. "I'll wash the windshield for you, if you want."

Catherine snugged her purse under her arm. "No, but thank you," she answered. Unnerved, she hustled into the diner, more than a bit ruffled.

As she entered the diner's door, Catherine startled to the *ho, ho, ho!* of the kitschy plastic Santa by the register. Rankled all the more, Catherine scanned the diner. Seeing her, Kiki approached.

"Hello," Catherine started. "I won't be dining. I just—"

At that moment, Merry exited the kitchen. Catherine quickly caught her eye. Merry waved congenially, then poured coffee for her customer.

Catherine glanced out the window, checking on her car. She spoke in confidential tones to Kiki. "I don't mean to... Is my car safe? That man out there, he—"

Kiki interrupted with a chuckle. "Skeeter? Oh, he's harmless."

"Well, would you mind keeping an eye out?" Catherine requested, handing Kiki a ten.

Kiki slyly accepted the cash. "Let's just ask him to."

With that, Kiki took Catherine's money and leaned out the front door, setting off the plastic

Santa's *ho, ho, ho-ing* yet again. "Hey, Skeet," Kiki called. "Watch this lady's car."

Skeeter lit up. "God bless ya, Miss," he called back. Realizing she was stuck, Catherine smiled tightly in return, just as Merry reached her.

"Catherine. What a surprise," Merry greeted, looking back out to the street. "Is Daniel coming?"

Catherine gathered herself. "He doesn't actually know I'm here," she replied.

♥   ♥   ♥

Daniel descended his living room stairs, a tiny wrapped gift box in his hand. There was something about seeing Ollie, amusing himself with the model train under the tree that warmed Daniel's heart. It reminded him of the joys of bygone Christmases and the promises of the ones to come.

As Daniel approached, Ollie played conductor, choo-chooing the string of cars around the track circling the Christmas tree.

Daniel stooped beneath the branches, adding the small box to the growing pile of gifts underneath. Reaching under a bough, he jostled one of Merry's broken china ornaments. Daniel looked at the creation with an affectionate grin, and then hid the ring box behind it, commenting to Ollie.

"Gramma's taking up some serious real estate with these packages here."

Ollie eyed the tiny package suspiciously. "Who's that little one for?"

Daniel checked around secretively, and then whispered to his son. "Let's keep it between us, but it's a very special gift for Catherine."

"From all of us?" Ollie inquired.

"In a way, but it's mostly from me," Daniel answered. "You like her, huh?"

Ollie shrugged. "She's okay, I guess. I like Merry better."

Daniel tipped his head. "I like Merry, too. But see, Ollie...I like Catherine in a different way. Kind of that man-woman thing. Like Mommy."

"Catherine's not like Mommy," Ollie answered.

"Well, no, but—"

Ollie jumped in definitively. "I like Merry. She's pretty, don't you think?"

Daniel scrambled for a response. "Yeah, Buddy. I do, but..."

Daniel trailed off. He examined his conflicted heart. How could he explain something to his nine year-old son that he couldn't entirely explain to himself?

"Catherine, she's really special, too," Daniel said, "and the thing is...well, I promised her first.

Now she's gotten her father's blessing about me. And you know how I always taught you that a promise is a promise?"

♥ ♥ ♥

Across town at the Downtown diner, Merry sat opposite Catherine, refilling syrup dispensers while Kiki and Arthur closed out. It wasn't that Merry wanted to give Catherine any less than her full attention, but Catherine had come to her fulltime workplace, a job Merry knew she needed to keep after the holidays.

Catherine looked at Merry directly. "I won't mince words, Merry. You're stealing my show."

Merry squinted a bit. "Come again?"

"Please don't be coy, Merry. I already know you're smarter than you come off."

A quizzical expression crossed Merry's face. "Thank you?"

"You're a Christmas Coordinator, not the Pied Piper, okay?" Catherine continued. "And I'm asking you as nicely as I know how to stop piping, because if you won't give me a chance, neither will those children."

Merry wiped a dribble off a bottle. "You can pipe up, Catherine. Pipe away."

"I won't compete with you, Merry."

Seeing Catherine's distress, Merry put the bottle down. Something in Merry's heart went out to Catherine. "Then, get in there. Take the stage solo. Show them what you've got."

"I would. I could," Catherine insisted. "But, thanks to you, everything's already been done."

Merry shook her head. "Oh, it's a long way from done. I've hardly even started on the Christmas Eve party."

Catherine reared back in frustration. "That's great. I'm sure this will be yet another charming extravaganza, putting me even farther out of my comfort zone, while drawing him hook, line, and sinker into yours."

"Catherine, I never meant to—"

Catherine put a hand up. "Okay, no. Stop. Do you think it's easy for me to say these things?" Her eyes misted as she continued; her regal voice broke. "I mean, maybe I'm wrong. Maybe I'm a totally insecure mess and completely off. So, please, Merry, do us both a favor. Tell me here and now that you feel nothing for Daniel, and I'll apologize this minute."

Merry stopped, a deer, caught in the headlights. She had never been a liar in her life, and she resolved in that moment not to become one. What in the world could she say? She shot up a prayer for words.

"Well..." Catherine pressed.

Merry took a breath. "My job is over in a couple of weeks. It's not like it matters."

"Of course, it matters," Catherine retorted. "It's the most sentimental time of entire year and there you are, Little Miss Spotlight. You've constantly got his eye."

Merry swallowed the lump in her throat. "But you've got his heart, Catherine. He loves you. I know it. Me, I'm like a snowflake—a little sparkle that's there one moment, and then the next I melt right away, completely forgotten. Trust me. He doesn't look at me the way he looks at you."

Catherine stared at Merry, suddenly speechless. Every ounce of guardedness left Catherine's face. "You've seen him look at me?"

Merry smiled encouragingly. "Kind of hard to miss." Merry saw a glimmer of hope as it lit in Catherine's eyes. It encouraged her to continue. "You're the one he wants, Catherine. I know it."

"Still," Catherine allowed, "I... If you could allow me a moment or two to shine at this...Christmas Eve Party you're planning."

"Okay," Merry nodded, "but it takes more than a moment or two to work up a good shine, you know. Might have to roll your sleeves up," she advised.

Catherine cocked her head back warily. "Meaning...?"

"Meaning, you could help me with it. Run the whole she-bang, if you want."

"But Christmas Eve," Catherine sputtered. "That's just around the corner, now."

"So, you might want to hop on it," Merry suggested. "That is, if you really want to—"

"No," Catherine interrupted. "I couldn't. "

"Couldn't or won't?"

Dejectedly, Catherine sat back in the booth. "I don't think like you, Merry. Sometimes I wish I did, because I don't want to lose him, but face facts. I'm not folksy. I'm not fun. I'd have no idea what to do."

Seeing Catherine's genuine despair, Merry pondered it, wrestling mightily with her heart. She could let Catherine flounder and allow things to take their natural course. Or, she could remember what the season was all about. She could be the larger person and do what she could to help.

Merry smiled warmly at Catherine. "We may be way different in a lot of ways, but you want to know how we're exactly alike? I really do know what it's like to be in a tough spot with no earthly idea what to do. So, maybe that's what I can give you for Christmas, Catherine," Merry offered. "An idea or two."

eleven

There was always something about the twenty-fourth of December that seemed every bit as special to Merry as the stage it set for following day. As the sun descended behind a blanket of winter clouds, a light snow began to fall, dusting the streets with the promise of a white Christmas. Anticipation filled the Bell household, for the first time in years. Merry knew that her job was essentially done. All that was left was to stand back and watch it unfold.

Strong Bank & Trust had closed early for the holidays, releasing Daniel for a well-earned week of vacation. Arriving at home, Daniel brushed the snow crystals off his coat as he entered the kitchen door. A look of surprise lit up his face to find Merry, his mother and kids, all dressed as elves in a makeshift assembly line. Busily, they stocked dozens of holiday bags with treats, gifts, and personal supplies.

"Whoa! What's this?" Daniel queried.

Ollie looked up from his work. "Duh. It's Christmas Eve, Dad."

"Yeah, try to keep up," Hayden quipped.

As Daniel took off his coat, Tara eyed his attire. "You're not wearing that, are you?"

Daniel glanced around, puzzled. "To what? I thought we were having our party here tonight."

"You said I could outsource," Merry reminded. "So, Catherine volunteered to throw together a little something." With a gesture toward the living room, Merry gave the floor to Catherine, who sashayed in wearing a darling Mrs. Santa outfit.

"Better run upstairs and put this on, Father Christmas," Catherine beamed, handing Daniel his costume on a hanger. "Your ride's coming in twenty minutes."

Soon, a carriage drawn by four horses sporting reindeer antlers clip-clopped through the snowy downtown streets. The Bell contingent snuggled under warm tartan blankets, caroling as they traversed the winter wonderland. Merry purposefully remained in the background as Catherine led the singing from a festive booklet of Noels.

As the sleigh pulled up outside the Downtown Diner, Merry gave Catherine an encouraging grin, seeing what she had accomplished. A *Merry Christmas* banner was festooned across the font awning, welcoming the neighborhood homeless. A long row of shopping carts, overflowing with the belongings of the area's transients, stretched along the walk.

When the Bells hopped out of the carriage and headed inside, Skeeter greeted them with a gentlemanly tip of a vintage top hat. Sporting a dashing cutaway, he "parked" another shopping cart neatly at the end of the line. The lady who owned it sifted through her belongings. "Lemme give ya something, Skeet," she said.

Respectfully, Skeeter waved her off. "No, Ma'am," he assured. He smiled at Catherine as she passed by on Daniel's arm. "Nice lady here's payin' me good to work this. Go on in. You're our guest."

Merry was the last to enter the diner. As soon as she did, she saw that the old *ho-ho-ho-ing* Santa had been replaced with a much nicer, more welcoming version, no doubt Catherine's doing. A trio played from the corner, filling the air with holiday cheer.

As she scanned the decorated diner, in some ways Merry's heart was breaking, but then again, it felt incredibly full. She was doing the right thing and she knew it.

In no time, the Bells were at their stations and the party was in full swing. Kiki and Hayden gave out festive headwear to arriving homeless. Each and every party guest was crowned with holly or stars, halos or antlers, just as soon as they walked in Arthur's door. Joan ladled hot chocolate and steaming cider to grateful street folk.

Merry headed to the kitchen just in time to see Catherine as she leaned down to serve holiday cookies to an elderly woman in a wheelchair. "Thank you, Darlin'," the old woman said with a toothless smile. "These look just like the kind my mama used to make!"

Merry pushed through the swinging doors and into the diner's kitchen where Arthur hustled to refill service trays with scrumptious treats. There were buffalo wings, stuffed mushrooms, fruit chutney, steamed shrimp, fancy cheeses, and hors d'oeuvres, the likes of which had never been tasted by this crowd. Catherine had insisted that they should have no less than she would serve at any other party she'd ever thrown, and Arthur had been game to deliver. Since Arthur had given her so much time off, Merry thought about how grateful she was that Catherine had decided to give him the business.

Through the open service window, Merry could see the whole family pitching in and having a wonderful time. Daniel and Tara passed out gift bags to each man, woman, and child who approached their table. Merry watched their guests revel over the great many surprises inside, no matter how small. To most it may have just been a hand towel, a comb, or a pouch of bus tokens, but to these people, the gift bags were a treasure trove. An indigent mom kissed the new toothbrush Hayden gave her. The woman's eight year-old son was thrilled to discover a pocket video game in his sack; a man paraded around to show off his new hand-knitted scarf.

As the night progressed, Merry filtered through the crowd, watching as downtrodden souls forgot their troubles and danced joyously to the music. Ollie kicked up his heels with a homeless girl, having the time of his life.

Skeeter bowed deeply in front of Catherine and extended his open hand. "May I have this dance?"

Merry noticed that Catherine was a little taken aback at first. But apparently, in an instant, Catherine thought better of it and offered Skeeter her hand.

"It would be my pleasure, Sir," Catherine answered.

As Merry loaded a fresh tray of goodies, Kiki elbowed her, eyeing Arthur. He was still busying himself with food preparation. Merry whispered that Kiki should go for it.

Kiki sashayed over to Arthur. "Got enough for three parties now," Kiki cracked. "Time for you and me to go have us some fun. You do know how to dance, don't you?"

Arthur looked up, confused. "You. Asking me. To dance."

Merry stifled a giggle.

Kiki exhaled dramatically. "Been asking you for most of fifteen years, case you ain't noticed."

Slowly a light dawned for Arthur. After all those years working side by side with Kiki, he was finally starting to get it. He pointed as he spoke, to make sure he'd understood. "You mean you. And me. Dancing."

"What do you think," Kiki sassed, "I been hanging 'round here all this time for the tips?" With that Kiki grabbed Arthur's hand and pulled him out of the kitchen.

As Merry passed by with her tray of treats, Daniel offered to take it for her. It was tempting to enjoy a moment with him, but Merry redirected Daniel's gaze to Catherine, dancing with Skeeter near the musicians. "I'll get this. Go. Try your moves."

Daniel obediently made his way through the crowd toward Catherine. Merry circled the perimeter and handed her tray to Joan.

"You doing okay?" Joan asked.

"How could I not be?" Merry covered. "Just look at everybody. They're having such a great time. Look at your granddaughter." Merry directed Joan's gaze across the room where Tara helped a middle-aged woman to try on a new tube of gift lipstick. Tara held up a mirror while the woman blotted her lips together, delighted with the results.

Arthur and Kiki cut a mean rug, capturing Merry's attention. It seemed now that Arthur could finally see Kiki, he could hardly take his eyes off her.

Merry took their pairing in with a bittersweet sigh. She was off the charts thrilled for them, but—truth be told it made her feel her own singleness all the more acutely. Merry shook it off, purposely turning her gaze to Hayden as she helped a few homeless kids toss wreaths onto candy cane striped posts for prizes.

Merry nodded across the room at Daniel, signaling him to go ahead. Daniel turned and politely tapped Skeeter's shoulder. "Mind if I cut in?"

Skeeter bowed out like the gentleman that he was, making way for Daniel to take Catherine into his arms. Indeed, they made a striking couple.

As the band transitioned to a slower tune, Kiki and Arthur spun right by Merry, nuzzling like old marrieds. Daniel swayed nearby with Catherine.

Merry watched it all from the sidelines. Shoving her pain inside, she retreated to the kitchen alone. With so much Christmas wonder going on, she couldn't bear to be thinking of herself, but the price she had paid in giving this gift to Catherine was almost more than her breaking heart could bear.

♥   ♥   ♥

Caught up in the moment, Daniel stopped counting his steps. He began to actually enjoy dancing with Catherine, and she couldn't have looked happier, swaying with him to the music. As much as he almost hated to admit it, Merry had been right, he thought. She'd been right that Catherine would enjoy dancing. She'd been right about his kids. She'd been right about absolutely everything.

Suddenly, though it was Catherine that he turned in his arms, in Daniel's mind's eye he flashed back to his dancing lesson, on his backyard patio with Merry. All over again, it was Merry he spun in his arms, lost in the brilliance of a thousand lights.

Catherine broke Daniel's reverie. "You've been holding out on me."

"What's that...?" Daniel asked, training his mind on the present.

"I never knew that you danced," Catherine remarked. "We should do it more often."

Daniel nodded, deep in thought. *Where had that come from?* Through the service window to the kitchen, he saw Merry working diligently by herself. What it was that had told him to hire her, he didn't really know. But he found himself thanking God that he had. In just a matter of weeks, she'd become a surprisingly meaningful part of their lives. It was hard to imagine that she'd ever been a stranger. He would miss her, he realized, when the holidays were over. So would the kids.

Exactly what it was about Merry, Daniel wasn't sure. In some ways, he found her so comfortable to be with, and in others she completely unsettled him. He hadn't hired her to do it, but something about her had made him question himself, since the first day she'd asked for the job. From the very beginning, she had pushed past the boundaries of professional service and into their still-grieving hearts. She had gone beyond the seasonal trappings of Christmas to the core of his family's need.

As he moved across the dance floor, Daniel watched his children. They were coming back to life again in ways that amazed him. Ollie wanted to connect with him in an entirely new way. Tara was maturing, becoming more selfless before his eyes.

SUSAN ROHRER

Even Hayden seemed to be forgetting her troubles. That dark cloud that had persisted for the past three years was finally beginning to break.

Despite Merry's unconventional approach, and probably because of it, she had been exactly what they'd all needed this Christmas. *How did she get to be so wise?* Merry had the gentlest way of leading him to answers that seemed to have been there all along, he pondered. And this evening, it seemed that she was leading him straight to Catherine.

♥　♥　♥

As all well-enjoyed parties must, the evening wound to a close. Merry watched through the service window as Catherine stood with Joan by the door, bidding each of their guests a fond good night. Meanwhile, the kids helped Kiki and Arthur to put the diner tables and chairs back into order on the service floor.

Merry turned to the kitchen sink. She began to wash a stack of trays, making peace with her lot. Having plenty to do always helped Merry, especially when things were hard. She did her best to concentrate on the task at hand, and to forget that her dream of a job was quickly coming to a close. Arthur had been right. What had gone up would soon have to come down, including her already plummeting hopes. She wondered how she would survive it, but trusted that somehow she would.

Daniel pushed through the swinging door with a large bag of trash. "There you are," he said. "Don't you want to say goodbye to everyone?"

Merry brushed an escaped tendril from her forehead. Staying in the background had been challenging all evening. Going out to enjoy the thanks of their guests seemed harmless enough, but the fact that Merry wrestled with whether or not it would draw attention from their hostess convinced her to opt otherwise.

"That's okay," she replied warmly. "It's Catherine's place. She arranged everything, you know. She's even bringing Christmas dinner over to you tomorrow."

Daniel studied Merry thoughtfully. "Funny. I wouldn't have guessed she had it in her."

"Never know what's inside a person, I suppose," Merry answered.

Daniel shook his head, his growing affection for Merry showing. "I don't know about you, Merry. You just seem to be able to bring out the best in everyone, don't you?"

"What's there is there," Merry said. "Just got to polish it up, so you can see it."

Daniel took it in, seeming to perceive more than Merry felt able to express. A moment of quiet understanding passed between them. Nothing was said, but then again, it seemed best to her that nothing would be.

Catherine leaned in the door. "The sleigh is here, Daniel. Merry, can we drop you?"

Merry turned to Catherine pleasantly. "Thanks, but no. I'll get the El."

Daniel lingered after Catherine headed out to the door. "You'll join us for church in the morning, won't you?"

Merry's eyes misted. It was all she could do to bridle her rising emotions. "I'm so glad you're all going, Daniel. And, believe me, I'd love to. But no. I just can't."

Snow continued to fall as Merry walked home from the station alone. It was late, but Mr. Grabinski was outside, shoveling the walk. A train rumbled by overhead.

Life was returning to normal.

"Merry Christmas, Mr. Grabinski."

The old super scowled as usual. "Not so much, if this keeps up."

Merry entered her darkened studio apartment and flipped on the light. Rudy stretched from his nap, happy to see her.

Merry picked Rudy up and scratched his neck. "Come here. You didn't think I'd make you spend Christmas Eve all by your lonesome, did you? Gotcha something."

Merry sat with Rudy and pulled out a catnip mouse. "You like it, boy?" She playfully moved it near his nose, and then teasingly drew it back. "What's this, Rudy? What's this?"

Rudy sniffed the catnip curiously. He pawed at it, and then carried it in his mouth to his pillow.

Merry took her coat off. She hung her elf hat on a hook. There, on the kitchen counter, was the little wind-up kangaroo that she'd bought for Daniel. Sadly, she put it back into its shopping bag. There was no way that she could give it to him now. It would make him think of her, she reasoned, and she knew that just wouldn't be right.

Merry wandered over to her little Christmas tree with the burned out lights and not a single solitary present underneath. Tears brimming, Merry tried to encourage herself. She looked out at the falling snow, quietly devastated.

twelve

Merry awakened to the light of the rising sun, sparkling on new-fallen snow. Though Rudy continued to slumber contentedly beside her, she crawled out of bed and padded to the window. Frost edged the panes in intricate patterns. The brightest of white blankets outside was enough to make even Merry's neighborhood look pretty.

Soon, Mr. Grabinski will be out front, shoveling the walk again, she thought. *Like always.* Across town, the Bells would be stirring from their beds. Before long, they'd be at their church, singing *Joy to the World*. They'd come home and open their presents. They'd sit down to eat Christmas dinner, like people who have families do together. They would make new memories. They'd start afresh, just as Daniel had wanted.

Merry inhaled deeply, contemplating her surroundings. This was her world. The Day of Days had arrived in all its shining glory, and for the first time in her life, something inside Merry was wistful about the fact that it had come.

It wasn't just that her Christmas Coordinator job was ending, Merry realized. It was much more than that. It was that tiny wrapped jewelry box she knew waited for Catherine, nestled in the boughs of the Bell's family tree. It was those Four Words, that question Daniel would ask Catherine when she opened it, the question Merry had begun to hope she would hear from him in time herself.

So this is it, Merry thought.

This is what it's like to be in love.

Never in her life had Merry known that feeling. She'd thought about what it might be like. She'd dared to dream that it could happen to her someday. But never in all Merry's wildest imaginings had it been like this: that she would be so in love with a man like Daniel, yet so utterly alone.

♥   ♥   ♥

Across town, Hayden yawned as Tara led her up the attic stairs to the landing. Ollie climbed up behind them, still in his pajamas. Hayden couldn't imagine what they were so anxious to show her or what could possibly be worth dragging herself out of bed for so early.

Hayden looked at the entrance to the attic quizzically. It was covered floor to ceiling with green foil wrapping paper. A broad red ribbon with an enormous bow stretched over a tag with Hayden's name. Hayden stared at it in shock. "This is my Christmas present?"

Ollie tugged at his sister's robe excitedly. "You gotta rip the paper off."

Hayden looked at Tara, who nodded her approval. With that, Hayden tore through the paper and into her new room. She scanned it, open-mouthed for the longest time. "Really?" Hayden could feel it as Tara watched her face for a response.

"You like it?" Tara asked.

Hayden stepped into the freshly redecorated space. In addition to a twin bed topped with fluffy pillows, there was a nice computer station. A comfortable seating area was set up beside the dormer window. "That's mom's rocker," Hayden observed.

Tara followed. "Yeah, kind of old-school. But I thought you could sit there, you know. Think about her. If you want."

Hayden turned to Tara, stunned. "You did this. For me."

Ollie stepped between them. "I was her elf. It's from me, too."

Touched beyond expression, Hayden hugged Tara tightly, grateful tears brimming. She made sure that she squeezed Tara longer and harder than she had since they were little girls, dressed exactly the same.

Ollie threw his arms around his sisters. He looked up at Tara jubilantly. "I think she likes it," he grinned.

Hayden knew that her new room was only the beginning of surprises in store for her family. She hung back, watching as the others opened their gifts. Her dad loved the new plates her Gramma had turned for him at her shop. And, in return, Gramma had seemed very pleased with the sweater-coat he'd asked Merry to choose for her.

It was fun to watch as Ollie tore into a mysteriously long package she had helped Merry to wrap for him. Though Ollie was clueless as to what it could be, Hayden couldn't wait to see his goofy little face when he realized what it was.

Peering into the box, Ollie's eyes bugged. He pulled out a fishing rod and reel, ecstatic. "We're going fishing?"

"Got that right," Daniel nodded.

Ollie jumped up and down, repeatedly. "We're going fishing!" he shouted, pumping the pole into the air with glee.

Hayden stood with Tara and Ollie, watching with anticipation as their dad opened his gift from them, a shiny red caboose to complete his train set. And just when the day seemed it couldn't get any better, Tara enthralled Ollie with gallon jar of wriggling worms to go with the tackle box Hayden had picked out for him.

As each gift was opened, Hayden glanced under the tree, near the back, at the package she'd wrapped for Tara. There were so few left. In a way, she was tempted to take the present back, run upstairs, and order a gift certificate for Tara instead. But how could she do something so impersonal after what Tara had given to her? Merry's words kept ringing in her ears, that the gifts that were the hardest to give were the best ones. That must mean her gift to Tara was great, she thought, because giving it was taking every ounce of strength that she had.

Hayden stalled, waiting till almost all of the packages had been opened. The only one left besides her gift to Tara was the little one her dad had nestled in the boughs, tagged for Catherine. Hayden hadn't asked what it contained. She didn't have to. She was pretty sure she knew exactly what it was and it was the last thing she wanted to think about. It wasn't that Catherine was so terrible. She was beginning to grow on her in a weird kind of way. It was just that the little box seemed like the only flat note in what was turning out to be a pretty decent Christmas, a better one than Hayden had expected it to be.

Finally, it happened. Ollie poked around the back of the tree. "Who's that one for?" he asked.

The moment of truth had come. Hayden reached under the tree and retrieved the package. As unceremoniously as she could, she handed it to Tara. "Okay, so it's not as Cucamonga-sized as your present to me, but...here you go."

Everything in Hayden squirmed as Tara tore off the wrapping, opened the box, and folded back the tissue paper. Inside was the sonnet Hayden had labored so long over, then matted and framed under glass.

Tara gazed at it, quite noticeably overwhelmed. *"To Tara,"* she read, as if she could hardly believe it. "You wrote your love sonnet about me?"

Hayden curled her lips into a crooked little smile. "I had to write it about somebody."

Her Gramma sat down beside Tara. "Read it, Honey," she prompted.

Tara handed the frame back to her sister. "No, you read it, Hayden. Please?" Hayden hesitated at first, then took a breath and began to read aloud:

"To Tara"

I wish I were the wonder that you are.
Perhaps you do not know how much I long,
To stand and shine alongside your bright star,
To find the vibrant hope that makes you strong.

Your face in my mirror, when e'er I glance,
Your voice, her heart, within resounds,
Leading by birthright, despite circumstance.
Resolved to conquer so much that confounds.

You are not yet so very much like her,
As I would hope and pray to someday be
But through the gift you are her mem'ry stirs,
Resurrecting life, through you, to me.

I fear to say what is so very true:
I love the sister that she gave in you.

Hayden couldn't bring herself to look up from the sonnet for the longest kind of time. In fact, it was all she could do to finish it. When she finally raised her eyes she saw that Tara's cheeks were also traced with tears. She saw her Gramma wipe her eyes, then reach over and squeeze her dad's hand.

Hayden handed the sonnet back to Tara sheepishly. "I only got a 'B' on it," she admitted. "Iambic pentameter got kind of funky."

Tara threw her arms around her sister. "I don't care," Tara cried. "I love you, too, Hayden."

Ollie looked around at his sisters, his misty-eyed dad and Gramma. "Why is everybody crying?"

Daniel pulled Ollie into a cheerful hug. "It's okay, Buddy. It's the good kind."

Just then, the doorbell rang. Daniel rose. "That must be Catherine."

Hayden flopped onto the sofa. "Fa-la-la-la-blah," she groaned.

♥ ♥ ♥

Before long, the Bell family had gathered around their festively decorated dining room table. Catherine backed through the door from the kitchen, carrying a perfectly browned turkey on a large platter. Joan made room on the table amongst dishes of steaming baby green beans, parsnips, and yams with browned marshmallows on top. There was chunky cranberry sauce, apple-pecan dressing, and a cut glass bowl of bright red watermelon rind pickles.

Daniel rose. "Catherine, let me help you with that."

"No, sit, sit," Catherine insisted. "This is my gift to all of you."

As soon as Catherine set the turkey down, Daniel broke into a grin. "Well, Mom...look at that," he remarked. "You made a new platter to pass down, didn't you?"

"I did," Joan nodded, pleased that Daniel had noticed.

"A vast improvement over the last one," Daniel added.

Ollie held up his matching plate. "I like our new dishes," he enthused, tracing his finger across the rim. "Look-it, they all have Merry's name right on them."

Catherine noticed that Joan stifled a smile as Ollie showed his dad how each dish was edged with holly along with the words *MERRY CHRISTMAS*, painted into the glaze.

Daniel gazed at the platter, making the connection. "Oh, look at that. I guess they do."

Catherine absorbed it pleasantly, doing her best to let their references to Merry roll off her arching back. "Daniel, would you like to do the honors?" she said, passing the cutlery set.

Hayden looked around. "Hey, where is Merry?"

"Yeah," Tara chimed in, "isn't this supposed to be her big day?"

"Yes," Catherine interjected, her discomfort growing. "That's why I told her I'd take care of things for her, so she could have some time to herself, and we could all enjoy Christmas dinner together."

Catherine couldn't miss the disappointment that flickered across each of the kids' faces. She coaxed herself to rise above it.

Ollie quickly appealed to his father. "But when is Merry coming, Dad? I want to show her the fishing rod you got me."

"And wait till she sees my sonnet," Tara said.

"And my room," Hayden added.

Tara turned to her twin. "Merry was totally in on that, you know."

Suddenly, a mortified expression crossed Joan's face. "Did anybody get her anything?" Joan searched around the table. Tara, Hayden, and Ollie looked at each other blankly. Catherine saw Daniel grimace, clearly mortified at the oversight.

"I gave her the day off," Catherine mentioned.

Hayden rolled her eyes. "How about something that she actually wanted? Face it. We're all total Scrooges."

Daniel shook his head. "No, it was my place. I should have thought of it."

Tara moped. "It's her birthday today, too. This is bad."

Ollie tugged at his dad's sleeve. "Let's call her, Daddy."

Catherine couldn't help interjecting. "I'm sure she'd much rather—"

Tara whipped out her cell phone. "Yeah, let's see if she'll come over."

"Oh, I know," Hayden said. "Put it on speaker and we can all completely grovel."

Tara's eyes lit up. "Or carol to her! She would love that. What's her number?"

Unable to take it any longer, Catherine flatly conceded. "555-7463."

Daniel turned to Catherine as she abruptly rose from the table, "How did you know—"

"If you'll excuse me," Catherine replied. Then, with as much dignity as she could preserve, she strode back toward the kitchen.

"What's with her?" Hayden asked.

Daniel pushed out his chair and stood up immediately. "No call to Merry just yet," he instructed. "Mom, could you carve, please?"

With that, Daniel quickly followed Catherine out of the room.

As soon as the kitchen door flapped closed behind her, Catherine burst into tears. When Daniel appeared, she tried in vain to dry them. Unable to hide her emotions, she quickly turned away.

"Catherine?"

"I'm fine," she whimpered. "I'm just... Who am I kidding? I'm a certifiable mess." Catherine threw her hands up in despair.

Daniel circled around her and faced her. "You look nice to me," he replied.

"That's just because I cry pretty," Catherine blustered. "Mother taught me never to scrunch."

Daniel nodded, beginning to understand. "This is about Merry, isn't it?"

"You think?" Catherine blurted. "It's not like I blame you. I mean, she's impossibly appealing. Even when she throws the ball completely into my corner, she's still the unwitting belle of it."

Daniel looked mystified. "What are you talking about?"

"Last night," Catherine admitted. "It was all her idea—every enchanting, infuriatingly generous bit of it—right down to hiring Skeeter."

Daniel reached out for Catherine's hand, but for the first time, she refused it. "Catherine..."

"I don't know why I can't do this," she mourned. "Sure. I can hold court with the best of society; I can schmooze with heads of state. But put me with a family and I'm completely out of my depth."

"They can't help loving her," Daniel explained.

"Oh, I know," Catherine replied. "Even I can't help it. The question is: can you?"

Daniel took the query to heart. When he finally opened his mouth to respond, Catherine cut him short.

"No, no. Please don't answer that," she said. "No. Let me just..." Catherine took a moment to gather her composure. "You know," she continued, "I've been thinking about things, and I realize we'd planned to exchange gifts tonight, but the truth is, if we did go through with all that, I...I suppose I'd miss my corner office." Catherine inhaled, rallying her poise. "Or travel," she mustered. "Yes. Maybe Paris. Or I might visit my ex in Rome. He sent me a lovely card this year and, well, quite by surprise, I find myself vaguely charmed, and wanting to at least give it a chance, explore the possibilities. Forgive me?"

Daniel nodded. He brushed Catherine's arm affectionately. It told her that he understood all that she couldn't bring herself to say.

Catherine removed her holiday apron. Her eyes glistening, she gave Daniel one last kiss on the cheek. "You'll say my goodbyes, won't you?"

"I will," Daniel assured.

Catherine picked up her clutch and crossed to the door. "My best to Merry," Catherine concluded, "when you see her."

♥ ♥ ♥

Night had fallen. Far across town, Merry set a dish out for Rudy, and then sat down to a bowl of clam chowder. Trying her best to be grateful, she bowed.

"So... Merry, here," she prayed. "Just me. Again. Sorry to be so droopy, especially today, but—"

The toot of a car horn outside interrupted Merry's thought.

Merry looked up as she continued. "I guess this wasn't exactly the Christmas I hoped it'd be." As she paused, remembering, a sheepish grin crossed her face. "But I didn't get evicted. And you did get me through it, like I asked. And it was good...good to see a family come together, even if it wasn't mine. So, thanks for letting me be part of it—"

Again, the horn blasted outside, twice in close succession.

"Thanks for Rudy, and this chowder and—"

Yet again, the horn blared, insistently. Merry glanced toward the window as she heard Mr. Grabinski yell toward the street. "Cut the racket, will ya? How's about a little peace on earth?"

Curious, Merry rose and went to her window, murmuring to herself, "What is...?" Merry looked outside toward the street. To her stunned delight, there stood the whole Bell family at the curb. Catherine was nowhere to be seen. Merry threw open the sash, overjoyed.

Seeing Merry in the window, Joan cued the family, and they all started to sing at the top of their lungs:

We wish you a Merry Christmas,
We wish you a Merry Christmas,
We wish you a Merry Christmas
And a happy New Year!

Merry listened, delighted. Though the sun had set, Christmas was suddenly far from over for Merry. It was only just beginning.

"Hi!" Merry called out. "Am I glad to see you! Come on up!"

Daniel stepped forward from the rest. "Not yet," he answered. "You come down first!"

It wasn't two seconds before Merry grabbed her coat and went bounding down the stairs. As she passed his first floor apartment, Mr. Grabinski poked his head out and yelled after her. "Would you keep it down?" he groused. "Some people trying to have Christmas, you know!"

As Merry burst out of her building, she could see the Bell family bubbling with excitement.

"Here she comes!" Ollie shouted. "Here she comes!"

Tara clamped a hand over his lips. "Shhh! Act natural."

Daniel prompted his kids. "Okay, get ready..."

Merry bounded across the snowy walk. She slipped gawkily, then regained her footing just in time to hear the whole clan shout out, in unison:

"Surprise!"

Merry skidded to a stop as the Bells presented a wrapped gift. She looked at the package, stunned. "You didn't."

Ollie nodded enthusiastically. "We did. We all made it. For your birthday."

"All of you...you made this?" Merry replied as she tore off the paper and opened the box. Inside, she found a framed family photo. It was the picture she was in from the Christmas tree hunt. She stopped to examine the frame, a gift in and of itself. It was a mosaic of their broken family china, put together in a beautiful new way. At the top, a banner read: *MERRY'S CHRISTMAS*. Tears sprang to Merry's eyes. "This is...it's like a family photo."

Daniel smiled fondly. "Yeah, it really is. "

Merry couldn't take her eyes off the picture. "Oh... I can hardly believe this," she said.

"Why are you crying?" Ollie asked. "Don't you like it?"

Merry hugged the boy tightly. "No, I love it. It's just...a really big first for me and...I don't even know how to—" Merry embraced Joan and Tara, then turned to Hayden. "Thank you so much! Thank you! Hayden, I know you don't do hugs much."

Hayden opened her arms. "I make exceptions," she said wryly.

Merry squeezed Hayden, then gazed at the family photo again. "This is the greatest present ever!"

Ollie tugged on Merry's sleeve. "Hey, Merry," he blurted. "You want to help me plant my worm farm?"

Merry feigned appropriate surprise. "Really? You got your worm farm?"

"Thanks to you," Daniel said, "we all got what we wanted for Christmas." Daniel's expression took on a hint of mischief. "Well, almost," he toyed. "There is one other thing I wanted to give you."

Merry beamed. She checked around to make sure he was actually referring to her as the Bell kids prodded their dad to give her his gift. Merry couldn't help being a little puzzled, seeing Tara link pinkies with Ollie.

Daniel stifled a shy grin, and then turned to his family. "I do believe there's a snowman just begging to be built around that corner."

The kids dutifully ran away, but Joan lingered momentarily.

"You, too, Mom," Daniel intoned.

Joan smiled knowingly, then followed the kids around the building. Daniel turned back to Merry, his eyes reflecting his heart.

Merry wasn't sure what to think. "You don't have to give me anything else," she said. "This photo is way more than I ever in a million years expected. What more could you possibly—"

Daniel put a finger to Merry's lips, stopping her. Everything in Merry tingled inside, but still she searched his face, confused.

Daniel scratched his head, adorably nervous. "You should know, I... I'll be returning that little trifle I'd bought for Catherine."

Merry's eyes widened. "You will?"

Daniel shrugged nonchalantly. "It caught my eye at first. But then, I realized it wouldn't have fit."

Merry gulped, hoping against hope that what seemed to be happening really was. "No?" Quietly, she thrilled as Daniel took her hand gently in his.

"I didn't see it at first," Daniel confessed, "But you were right. Because, when I look at your hand in mine, now, I find there's no comparison."

Tears welled in Merry's eyes as she found herself in Daniel's. "You see me, now."

Daniel nodded softly, never breaking her gaze. "I see you." He reached up to brush a tear off her cheek. "Don't cry," he whispered.

Merry smiled through her tears. "Sorry. I'm just so happy."

"Really?" he teased. "This is happy?"

Merry caught her breath. "I'm new at this," she admitted. "But yeah. I think so."

"There is one more thing," Daniel said. "All of the gifts and decorations you coordinated, they were great, all the ornaments you hung on the tree. But I realized just this afternoon that you seemed to have forgotten to hang one very special thing."

Daniel reached into his pocket and pulled out a small sprig of mistletoe, tied with a red satin ribbon. "Merry Christmas, Merry," he said.

Time didn't stand still at that moment, but somehow it seemed to slow for Merry. It was as if everyone and everything else faded into the sheer bliss of the night. Gone was the noise of the El, rumbling by on the track above them. There was no Mr. Grabinski grumbling about snow on the walk. There were only two people, discovering each other in a whole new way with all of heaven shining on them.

Merry savored every instant as Daniel raised the mistletoe above her head and drew her close. She melted his kiss, drinking in what she'd always wanted most of all. This was no quick act of fondness, she realized. This was the beginning of a whole new life. It was the tender expression of awakening love.

Suddenly, Daniel and Merry found themselves being pelted with snowballs. Breaking away, Daniel stooped to grab a handful of snow. "You don't know what you've started," he warned his kids.

"Do you?" Merry countered, packing a snowball of her own.

"I'll take my chances," Daniel grinned.

Jauntily, Merry took aim and hurled a snowball smack into Ollie's chest. The twins quickly retaliated.

Even Joan gamely took up the charge. With four against two, Daniel and Merry quickly found themselves completely outnumbered. It wasn't long before they playfully surrendered, overwhelmed with the wonder of it all. Christmas had come back to the Bell family, in all its hope and splendor, and it was a miracle to behold.

Twelve days later, Merry reflected on all that had transpired. In a way, it had been just as Arthur had said it would be. The baubles and boughs Merry had put up had indeed come down. The ribbons and music of the season had been stored for another year. The potted Christmas tree, stripped of its ornaments, was out back in the Bell yard, awaiting a place to grow.

The whole family gathered around as Daniel pitched a last shovel of earth out of a large hole he'd dug outside the study.

"That should do her," Daniel said. "See there, Mom? Right outside your new window."

Joan looked puzzled as Daniel pointed to his study. "My new... You mean your office?"

"I mean your room," Daniel clarified. "If you'll have it."

Finally understanding, Joan lit up. "Well...let's get this thing planted," she enthused. "Sounds like I've got packing to do!"

Merry and Joan lifted the balsam fir from its pot and settled it into its new place in the ground. Tara, Hayden, and Ollie scooped dirt around the base to cover the roots.

Hayden looked up at her father as she patted the dirt down. "Mom would have liked this, you know."

Daniel smiled in return. "Oh, yes," he said. "I think she would."

Ollie shielded his eyes, peering up at the top of the tree. "How big do you think she'll get, Dad?"

Daniel put an arm around Merry. "We'll just take care of her. See how she grows."

Merry took Daniel's hand in hers, content in his warm embrace. Bits of happy chatter wafted from the yard, carried by the crisp winter air, hinting at the promise of the future.

"Hey, remember the time I busted all the good family china?" Ollie chortled.

"Smithereens!" Tara shouted, her giggles infecting them all.

"Or when Merry fell off the Christmas tree?" Hayden snorkled.

Daniel drew back in mock indignance. "Hey, now. She was slippery!"

"Or, or, or, um..." Ollie sputtered. "Remember when my worm farm got loose?"

Hayden smacked her little brother, agape. "No way!"

"They didn't!" Daniel blustered.

"No, not yet," Ollie assured.

Her eyes dancing, Merry tousled Ollie's hair, adopting all of them in her heart. "Oooh, maybe not yet," she imagined, "but wouldn't that be fun?"

About the Author

Susan Rohrer is an honor graduate of James Madison University where she studied Art and Communications, and thereafter married in her native state of Virginia.

A professional writer, producer, and director specializing in inspiring entertainment, Rohrer's credits in one or more of these capacities include: a screen adaptation of *God's Trombones;* 100 episodes of drama series *Another Life;* Humanitas Prize finalist & Emmy winner *Never Say Goodbye;* Emmy nominees *Terrible Things My Mother Told Me* and *The Emancipation of Lizzie Stern;* anthology *No Earthly Reason;* NAACP Image Award nominee *Mother's Day;* AWRT Public Service Award winner (for addressing the problem of teen sexual harassment) *Sexual Considerations;* comedy series *Sweet Valley High;* telefilms *Book of Days* and *Another Pretty Face;* Emmy nominee & Humanitas Prize finalist *If I Die Before I Wake;* as well as Film Advisory Board & Christopher Award winner *About Sarah.*

As an author, Rohrer has published two non-fiction books: *The Holy Spirit: Amazing Power for Everyday People* and *Is God Saying He's The One?: Hearing from Heaven about That Man in Your Life. Merry's Christmas: a love story* is a print adaptation of Rohrer's original screenplay.

Other Books by Susan Rohrer:
ಹ ♥ ಈ

Nonfiction:

THE HOLY SPIRIT:
Amazing Power for Everyday People

IS GOD SAYING HE'S THE ONE?
Hearing From Heaven
About That Man in Your Life

Fiction:

VIRTUALLY MINE: a love story

♥   ♥   ♥

Recommended Romances:

NEVER THE BRIDE: a novel
by Cheryl McKay & Rene Gutteridge

FINALLY THE BRIDE:
Finding Hope While Waiting
by Cheryl McKay
(*non-fiction companion to Never the Bride*)

Printed in Great Britain
by Amazon.co.uk, Ltd.,
Marston Gate.